Ex-Members

Tobias Carroll

Astrophil Press
at University of South Dakota
2022

Astrophil Press at University of South Dakota
1st pressing 2022

Library of Congress Cataloging-in-Publication Data
Tobias Carroll
p. cm.
 ISBN: 978-0-9980199-9-4 (pbk. : paper)
  1.Fiction, American
Library of Congress Control Number: 2022930058

http://www.astrophilpress.com

ONE

PACKED CHURCHES

(2006 & LATER)

1

THE TOWER STOOD TALL near the banks of the Delaware, its simpatico skeleton birthed from the dream of a hotel. The name of the dreamer had been lost to memory, to a failure of public records, to ghosts in the walls with ill intent. It jutted into every westward gaze conducted in the nearby town, forming risible static in views of the setting sun, like the body of some mammoth saint left rotting for penance or remembrance. Glance at it offhand and it seemed an artifact from some other now; glance at it offhand and you might not think of it as the repository of failure and fragmentation, but as something lost and innocuous. But offhand glances rarely came. Even in this half-finished state, the tower was a proper landmark now, and had been so for a while.

For a few years the citizens of New Dutchess watched as the building came together, first foundation and then structure, and waited for the skeleton to become anything more. They walked and drove past the construction site. Those who made their way up or down the river could see it from there, like the walls of some medieval city that a fool had stacked atop each other rather than allowing them a proper sprawl. For a few years the citizens of New Dutchess walked and looked up and waited. The process of building never quite seemed to pause, but nonetheless it seemed to stagnate, a scar that never healed. The citizens of New Dutchess asked questions, and eventually investigations were promised, first at the level of the beleaguered municipal government, and then at the level of the beleaguered county government. The promised investigations had been conducted, the citizens heard one day. The headline was below the fold on a thin local paper, and the followups were relegated further back still. The dedicated few who followed the story read about tax shelters and investors still clinging to the dream of something being built on that spot, being completed on that spot. They dreamt of the summoning of a hotel, and of all that that might bring. They dreamt of a better future.

Instead they got the outline of a hotel that loomed over them, loomed over their town, loomed over the river. Children born with it looming began calling it "the tower," because that name seemed more accurate than those brief moments when their parents called it "the hotel." It was no hotel. It was nothing yet. It was frozen potential, and so the tower became a point of reference for the daughters and sons of New Dutchess, New Jersey, from the middle of the 1970s onwards. Meet me near the tower, the children would say. Fifteen stories tall, a highway nearby, no railroad to be found. Meet me near the tower, or in the woods near the tower, or outside the parking lot beside the tower that had been finished on time, that had come to something, that did serve a purpose.

There were, of course, periodic campaigns to raze the tower. There were periodic attempts to redevelop it, to kickstart that old broken hotel dream into a new shimmering hotel dream, or an office dream, or a residential dream. Hope never quite died down in some quarters of New Dutchess. If some company could be lured there; if some contract could be secured. If that skeleton could be brought to life, if that difficult birthing could be unpaused and turned into something bold and illuminating. Whole municipal administrations cursed the tower even as they latched themselves to it, seeking greater glory.

The tower, as always, was impassive. When the summonings failed, the tower still stood. When the children looked up at it bewildered, the tower still stood. Security guards waited outside of it and looked up and shrugged, the tower still stood. Police made periodic passages past it seeking defacement or defilement, the tower still stood. When those whose jobs had failed because of it cut their hands and ran them down the sides of concrete, the tower still stood. The children who'd first seen it loom over them conjured their myths about it and grew to adulthood and never quite shook those myths, those legends, the stories of what had gone wrong, of what had stunted the tower, of what had made it inert. The tower still stood. In 1985 Hurricane Gloria met New Jersey, and the tower still stood. In 1991 a nor'easter flooded parts of the town, and the tower still stood. And on nights some years later when thunder crashed and lightning lit up the western sky, a man named Virgil Carey sat on his front porch and let himself become half-drenched and looked up at his view of the tower and wondered if it would be so bad if, on one of these night, some storm finally brought the whole fucking thing down.

2

ON A SUNDAY EVENING IN THE SPRING, Virgil Carey set out from his house to take in a program of choral music at an Episcopal church three-quarters of a mile away. He would walk there, he decided. It was a walk that he could make. The distance seemed manageable, and the weather was pleasant. It was a day situated in the small window of proper spring bestowed upon the state for a few weeks each year. The sidewalks, Virgil saw, were clear. He would walk slowly. He would walk in a stately manner. He would give himself an hour for the trip from his front door to the church's entryway. An hour, he thought; an hour to walk most of a mile without sweating or stumbling, without his legs feeling chafed or brutally sore before his return trip had been undertaken. Virgil Carey was not in the best health of his life. Perhaps this walk would rejuvenate him, he thought. Perhaps it would bring him a sort of physical clarity.

He looked at the circular thermometer hanging from his front porch. He had bought it weathered; it was the sort of item that came with falsified age, as though it had been pulled from a hole leading to some other, simpler decade. He liked its look on this corner of the house. Another sat on his back porch; another could be seen from his bedroom window. It was sixty-five degrees. Warmer than Virgil would have liked for his first walk of this distance in years. But still. He wondered if he would be suffused by his perspiration by the time of his churchside arrival. And then, acting the devil's advocate, he wondered if he should carry a light jacket instead. The temperature was sure to drop following sunset, and the choral program was due to last for at least two hours.

Virgil ran the side of his left thumb across the top of the same hand's middle finger. There, he felt a spot that seemed numb, had been numb ever since the previous day when he'd carried some sacks full of dirt from the edge of the backyard to a garbage can resting beside the garage. The patch of skin tingled, as though a scar was waiting on some cue to begin to form. Virgil imagined rubbing it, imagined the tip snapping off, like a clove of garlic falling away from the rest of the pale mass.

But then, fingers and toes had always taunted Virgil. He remembered being seven, of looking at the soles of his father's bare feet one day as they rested upon the couch. Virgil saw cracks in them, lips of dead skin gone bone-white. He saw a potential handhold, took his fingers to it, and tugged. "Don't do that," his father said with a start. "It's impolite." Virgil had nodded, had never touched the feet of his father after that, but he continued to stare for several years that followed. There, in the area where he'd torn some of that skin away, he saw fresher skin revealed below. Younger skin, he thought. He wondered once if that was the secret, if that was some miracle that he had uncovered: if you could peel away skin and reveal someone younger. He imagined a younger version of his father revealed to him. He imagined his mother reduced by a decade or more.

At some point, the idea of that miracle had left him. But now, he looked at his own feet some mornings before the shower, or before bed, and he saw that same flaking, decades later, and he wondered if he might reveal some other version of himself. Younger, wiser, sharper, better. Some mornings, he took ahold of the loose flaps and he pulled, wondering if that day might be the one where a suburban transubstantiation was manifest. Wondered if he might slough off all of his bad decisions and regrets, undoing his old and recent flaws.

Virgil poked at the tip of his finger again. Nothing fell off, nothing broke through. He sighed and stepped off the porch, making his way towards the sidewalk.

On a Friday night in the early days of winter, Dean Polis stood beside a dozen musicians, facing a crowd of eight hundred in a cathedral on Manhattan's Upper West Side that had gone secular for the evening. Arrayed beside him were two laptops and a pair of samplers. The audience's presence was more than a little terrifying for him to behold. It was not a uniform crowd: Dean had watched some of them enter, and guessed that a span of fifty years sat between the youngest attendee and the oldest. There was history in that span, Dean thought. He tried to avoid thinking too much about it.

He was not unaware of the media attention; he read his reviews. Well, he read most of them. He saw Arthur Russell's work cited by more than a few, and he saw Gavin Bryars's name cited by a handful, and he felt warmly towards that handful. He had been sent some copies of his latest LP; he had hoped that they would not bear a sticker on the front with some cloying press quote and mention that a download code could be found within. The stickers were there, along with the quote: "Polis seamlessly ushers the baroque into the twenty-first century." That had not been his aim. Still. Eight hundred strong. Dean Polis, standing there, before the crowd, clad in most of a bespoke suit.

Dean had not wanted to stand in the front. In rehearsals, he had resisted for as long as he could. "I'm a musician, not a conductor," he had said. (And in the background, he heard one of the French horn players say, "Singer, I thought," and wondered if he'd also been at an Alphanumerics show in years past. Strange where people from then turned up.) You don't have to conduct, someone said. You just have to lead the group. You've done that before. And he had. Most of his previous performances had been smaller groups; truth be told, he preferred the solo performances: Dean and electronics, Dean and samples, Dean and a few notes sparingly arranged.

Somewhere along the way, the group had become tight. Not punk-band tight, not the tightness of five weeks on tour, but the rehearsals had worked well enough. And now he stood, the suit's vest over a shirt with its collar left a button more open than had been wise. A sudden reticence entered him, an anxiety that the edges of one sleeve might touch something and trigger sound from a laptop, or summon some sample before its time.

String players sat on either side of him. Behind him was a group of men and women bearing horns, and behind them were a trio of percussionists. He felt them all there, sitting and standing, all waiting for his signal. "Cornish in Mourning" was the name of the piece they were about to play. It had run forty minutes in the rehearsals. It was the longest single work he had ever been a part of. Surely some sets had run longer: his old band's final one, for instance, all of then with sweat bursting from their bodies and near collapse, wringing one more song, then another, and then a third out into the air. Dean remembered the song after that: the last last song they'd ever play. Dean remembered the borrowed guitar he'd carried for the last few songs; he remembered the cords in his neck feeling unfamiliar and structural. He remembered letting the guitar fall numbly to the stage and both hands connecting with the mic stand and his mouth going to it and a keening pouring out. He remembered the sound of the guitars coming from behind him, hitting him like the breaking of waves, the best impact he'd ever felt. He remembered wondering just what could come next.

Dean stood facing the audience. Conservatory-trained musicians were his band for the night. The audience awaited his work. His first step would be to summon a sample: a small ignoble sound over which a quartet of strings play, sparking "Cornish in Mourning"–the strings and the horns and the trembling drums and the voices. Dean felt the string players' eyes on him. Cody on the viola seemed in particular to be piercing his face with her eyes. And so Dean lowered his finger onto the key and waited for the sound to come.

Virgil Carey briefly stopped his walk at a mailbox. He slipped a padded envelope containing a cassette inside and continued on his way. Five slow blocks from there he heard his own breath come, a shortened sound. It was as though he he was his own neighbor. Virgil felt his pulse throb out through his face and diffuse into the air. He remembered walks in the cold after old shows; he remembered stepping out steaming with sweat after some hall show or basement show had run its course. He thought about taking up running. He had taken up running a year after he had moved into the house. Three blocks into his first run, he heard a strange sound, something uncanny and grotesque, and then realized that the sound was wheezing, and then realized that the wheezing came from his own mouth. That had been it for the running; he had slowed to a slow walk, continued for one more block, and then stopped. He put his hands on his knees and let the wracked sounds come from his throat until a more respectable coughing began.

He wondered if he might see any neighbors on his walk. He only knew a handful of them, even after five years in the house. There were no block parties or social events here, and Virgil didn't go out much. He recognized the local children from Halloween; he knew the silhouettes of certain neighbors who walked their dogs. General outlines were, for some, the best that he could do. Some nights he sat on the porch, sure, but he preferred to be inside. He often remembered driving through this corner of the town when he had been a teenager. One of his friends had lived in a house four blocks from what was now Virgil's home, and Virgil would often be his ride to various shows and trips to the closest movie theater. Sometimes, when he was younger, he would find the right record and drive through the neighborhoods where his friends lived and wondered what he might see: artifacts of memory or precursors to scandal, instances of recollection or moments of reconciliation. These days, he stayed closer to home. He hoped for visions, hoped for the sound of a ringing phone.

Virgil's house was largely anonymous. Plans to personalize it had never come. Sometimes, when he would walk through it, he had the sense that it was a house full of guest rooms, a place awaiting friends or family to spend the night. (None came.) He had hoped that Dean might, or Åsa, or one of his old dot-com coworkers. Circumstance had been his enemy on some counts. He himself had been his enemy on others.

He had the idea one day that he should find a box of his old zines and dismember them and wheat-paste the pages across bedroom and office walls. He would take old flyers from VFW halls and basements and venues that popped up in college towns. He knew he'd see the name of the Alphanumeric Murders on there, time and time again, and thought that he might not put those flyers up. Not yet. There would be many more. A punk rock boutique hotel, he thought. He laughed as he walked and hoped it didn't sound like a wheeze.

Usually when he went to the church he drove. He was unsure if he had found some faith or if he simply craved company. It was a recent decision, still unformed, but he felt decent about it. His moments there on Sundays were some of the few in which he was around others. There might be a brief moment of shaking another hand; there was a sense that he wasn't alone in the world. Some days, he did have that sense. He would occasionally sign for a delivery or encounter a political canvasser or smiling savant looking to save his soul. Two sentences of conversation; perhaps three. It was the same with supermarket cashiers: he opted for late-night purchases, the stores open all night a fifteen-minute drive away. He wondered what they thought of him. He hoped nothing bad, on his best days. There were nods to the cashiers and nods to his fellow post-midnight shoppers, but otherwise, he might as well have been mute. Even in the church, he slipped out at service's end. He would go for the services, but not for anything more social than that.

Still, there was talk of fellowship that Virgil heard from time to time. He understood that it had a mystical quality to it. He understood that this was, for the moment, what stood between himself and utter isolation. Virgil wondered if he might not continue these walks. If he might not eventually introduce himself to someone; if he were not yet that far gone. He remembered other walks–largely down sidewalks in New York, but also through the older parts of New Dutchess, the parts that came before a suburban boom, when a centrality was assured. He remembered walking the Coney Island boardwalk, the sound of the ocean churning in one ear and the feel of splintering boards through the thinning soles of his shoes. He remembered drives and elation on streets not far from here. He remembered Panos calling him from Cape May, talking rituals and exhortation and divination. Virgil felt that sense of dislocation now, a sudden dizziness, a sense that he was witnessing his own body from a remove, from an observation tower, from a point of control.

He should call Panos, he thought. Panos might have stabilized again, settled down, turned his extremity back into eccentricity. Panos had had a fondness for renaming spaces and devising new sorts of maps: there was a space in Newark dubbed The Anchorage, a space in New Hope christened The Last Oak, and spaces in Rutland that were called Argus and Mitchell and Weronika. Virgil had learned of the Vermont sites through pictures sent through the mail. He had spoken to Panos not long afterwards and had received a long lesson in the pronunciation of "Weronika." He missed Panos's manias; he missed the strange ebbs and flows of their friendship, unlike any other he had had, even in its fraying.

As he walked, Virgil saw houses, some nearing a century in age; moderate lawns and brick chimneys jutting out over flat roofs; impeccably painted white shutters; sedans and hatchbacks and restoration projects, covered for the inevitable bad weather. Virgil felt something catch in his throat and realized that, yes indeed, the wheeze had caught up with him. Were there to be tears as well? He paused to catch his breath and wished he had carried water, then wondered how the strange numb spot would have felt against plastic. He thought of the music behind him and the music that awaited him, ready to be sung into the world.

Dean had dubbed himself "an accidental composer" in an interview eighteen months earlier, and that description seemed to have stuck. He didn't mind. He had learned to read music as a child, and it had stayed with him. He had notebooks from his punk days where he'd sketched out short fragments, studies, meditations. Once on tour in the middle of Montana, he had sprung awake in the van's back seat with a realization of how he might unite two seemingly disparate motifs. He had looked around him, seen the familiar shapes of the van, and exhaled brilliantly, an unshakeable smile on his face. This was a new form of elation, and he savored it.

Sometimes these moments of inspiration came, and sometimes they abandoned him, leaving him as blocked, simply further along in the process. He enjoyed it sometimes, the chase through notebooks and pages and post-its, the hunt for brilliant fragments in the wake of his past inspiration. And then, the first furtive recordings, hidden away from anyone else. And the gradual handing off of some of the recordings to those closest to him, still a kind of secret. But still: he was a better composer than he was a musician. He had clung to a guitar for the last year or so of Alphanumerics shows, true, but that was the last push, that was the last attempt, that was the final way that they might confound expectations.

The music he wrote outpaced the music he was capable of playing, and from that gulf came an unease in actually handing his music

off to others to play. Not then, anyway. He wrote more, first in apart-
ments in and around New Dutchess and then on the Lower East Side.
And then, after the divorce, in assorted Brooklyn neighborhoods. He
looked out windows and felt something grow in him, his enthusiasm
for this secret pursuit quickening his heart even as frustration birthed
a cyclical resentment. He would glare at the notes. He worried he
might alarm passers-by. Sometimes that inner loathing took him over
and stayed his hands, and sometimes it drove it further.

Slowly his work emerged into the open. The path from there
to here, to this church, to the musicians arrayed around him now
enmeshed in the music that he had written, in "Cornish in Mourning." He flipped his eyes up to the audience and just as quickly moved
to the papers on a stand before him. No more looks out, he thought.
This was a new energy, and it both unsettled and elated him—not from
pride, but from the thrill of uncertainty of where this all might go. He
hoped for more curiosity in the amassed crowd, that that would be
the dominant mood. He knew there were pockets of skepticism out
there somewhere, people who considered him a pretender, someone
without the right to be there. He would probably be skeptical as well,
for his own reasons. The biography that he had made his own seemed
unlikely. But still, here he was.

He felt the strings sweep up to a dissonant pinnacle. He enjoyed
those moments of dissonance, had enjoyed them coming from four-
pieces with guitars, and enjoyed them even more now that he could
make them emerge from a group such as this. He craved the dizziness
they inspired, and hoped he would not be swept up in it. Dean stood
ready, finger awaiting the signal, prepared to trigger the composition's
first voice.

Virgil's church was now in sight. The steeple rose about a monotonous
treeline like the prow of a sinking ship. He was still blocks away, he
knew, and the bitter sweat summoned by the walk brought percus-
sive blinks to his eyes. His legs felt odd, like cinder blocks mounted
to tree branches, each step a delicate maneuver, carrying with it the
fear that he'd hear something snap. He wasn't supposed to feel this
ersatz yet; it was a brittle feeling that seemed decades away. Virgil

reached up to swipe sweat from his brow and from one cheek. He felt the skin of his hand recede. His fucking cushions, he thought. Some cut-rate cartoon character's gloves. The skin around his fingers' last joints was still taut. He wiped the sweat that remained on his pants and worried for a moment that their color might be despoiled by stains. Junior-high talk of swampass flooded back after twenty years. Bodies bewildered him.

Three blocks to the church now. The distance seemed tolerable.

He had begun going there late the previous year. He remembered his father's voice over the phone: "You might meet people." This was code for date, and they both knew it. He thought it might be calming. The first time he went, he sat in the back and watched. He stood when he had to stand but never knelt, never approached the altar. During the first ten minutes of the service, he had felt a stirring, and with it came an unlikely elation. Perhaps this was what old friends experienced when they turned to religion, he thought. Perhaps this would be a sort of rebirth for him, too.

And then, ten minutes later, he began to recognize the sensation even more, to see what it truly was. It was itself a kind of recognition; it was the familiar parts coming back to him, the same words he'd heard every weekend as a child, those rituals embedded in his body. This was like digging out old records, or going to some band on their reunion tour. This wasn't spiritual; it was muscle memory. After that first service, Virgil considered his place there. He could think of nothing better to do, though; the idea of investigating other spaces exhausted him. He understood nostalgia full well in that moment, understood why bands reunited and why audiences went out to see them. He had a Sunday routine now, even if he was far from a believer.

The middle section of "Cornish in Mourning" began with a barrage of plucked strings. Three distinct rhythms shifted in and out of sync with one another. Sometimes, the effect was chaotic, a chorus of linotype machines enmeshed in quarrel. Sometimes, major-chord calm arose out of the furious dialogue, creating a sense of solemnity, of arguments at a wake abruptly giving way to grief. Dean remembered writing this section. In many ways, it has been the most difficult part of the composition. For a long time, the music as it was written had stalled, circling around within its own structure. He had spent two months staring at it without a breakthrough. A casual suggestion had gotten him part of the way towards motion, but he remained bogged down for another two months, staring at measures written out in notebooks, trying different orchestrations. He ran the same themes through keyboards, through guitars, through brass and strings; the result was the same.

He had opened a second notebook to take down impressions, to write statements of purpose, to approach the muddle from all sides and see from what ways it could be resolved. He remembered years before, standing in a humid venue in Philadelphia watching a band play a furious instrumental set. There were numerous drummers, each playing a part that wove in and out of the other's. Dean stood in the back of the venue, first watching, taking in the entire experience, and then breathing deeply, focusing in on the rhythms, focusing in on just how each part fit with the others. He traced the way the drumbeats accelerated. He waited, as each minute advanced the cause of the music's climax, which was never attained–there would be an approach and an aversion, again and again. And after a while, Dean realized that that peak would never come. Dean felt hoaxed. And, though he would never admit to it except to a few close friends, he had written "Cornish in Mourning" as a kind of response to that night, his own accelerated cacophony, but one with a resolution.

In this way, Dean had quantified his disappointment. All that was left to do, then, was to understand why it had disappointed, and how it might have gone right–how that promise might be salvaged. Finally, he understood what he was writing against, and how he might push against it. The solution came in a couple of hours late one night, the phasing of the drums slowly falling apart, never losing its regularity, and the strings coming in.

Dean stood beside the musicians and heard the strings that he had summoned. A long droning section would soon come, a slow melodic progression. It sounded strange from where he stood, the reverberations from this position in the church making the accentuations all wrong. He wondered about the crowd, wondered how they were taking it. A fifteen-foot gap separated him from the front row of the audience. He thought about intimacy. It had been far too long since he had last been part of an audience.

For a moment, he wished he had written himself more to do here: more samples to trigger or voices to summon. The strings played the beginning of the final movement, a four-note progression. Dean waited for the silence to follow, and then the sound of the horns, picking up that nascent melody and creating a warm tone from it, then shifting it elegiac. Two French horns and two trumpets hit that first resonant note and held it. If he could distill this piece down to its essence, it would be that note, he thought—and then reconsidered. Perhaps the palimpsest of "Cornish in Mourning" was still to come. He looked out at the faces facing him and reconsidered the piece in a hundred ways. For a brief moment, he missed his time in basements, in VFW halls, in sweaty bunkers on summer tours.

On a familiar Friday night in winter, Åsa Morgan stood in the back of a church and heard the sound of an old friend's music. She stared out over the audience, watching Dean Polis in the role of bandleader, watching the small ensemble making music in modular groups. She waited for it to come together, and found herself, against her better judgment, being slowly drawn in.

Virgil Carey's legs were beyond sore by the time he entered the church. He felt a tenderness in his inner thighs. Tomorrow would bring tender steps, he knew. The entrance to the church loomed above him, the fifteen-foot doors it was made to hold flung open, letting in the air. Instead of the greeters he saw for the Sunday morning services, Virgil beheld a table with a folding chair behind it, and a man sitting there with a metal cashbox. Virgil handed the man twenty dollars and got a halfhearted sort of ticket stub in return. Virgil nodded and walked further inside, wondering just how visible the leavings of his sweat was. The church was old: nearly two hundred years had passed since its first beams were put into place.

The space, Virgil saw, was about two-thirds full. Mostly, the attendees were couples of his parents' generation; there were handful of faces a decade younger than his as well looking earnest, scattered throughout the room. He assumed they were college students, living south and east of here. Conservatory kids, he thought. Briefly, he imagined a strange balance in the parking lot: half resounding sedans and half weathered subcompacts, college stickers covering up cracks and scratches in the latter's bumpers. It was the reverse of the migrations Virgil and his friends had made as they drove away from New Dutchess in their late teens, bound for hardcore shows elsewhere in the state and in corners of Pennsylvania and Staten Island.

He saw sweat seeping through his shirt and realized that he was not far from a seat. It brought a kind of comfort. Still, his heart hammered, and a slow regret distended his stomach as he realized that sitting here wouldn't stop the sweat, that he would leave moist outlines of his form on the wood, that he would bring a kind of disgrace to the area in which he sat. He hoped he didn't stink. He hoped he wouldn't leave a sort of radius of space around him. Virgil hated being conspicuous.

The aches trickled throughout his body, and he thought for a long time about the best way he could get home. At least he wasn't wheezing as he sat. He could call a car, he knew. He could ask some acquaintance in attendance for transportation. But there was shame in that for him as well. He looked around the room but saw few faces that he recognized; of those, there were none of people with whom he was close. He could ask, he knew. It was a facet of the community. When he'd been a kid, when he'd gotten rides to shows in basements and halls, he had done such things many times. There was an implied trust. Here, there was only potential disgrace. He understood his appearance. He understood that it was unseemly of someone in their thirties to ask a stranger for a ride home, even in a church, even now. He didn't resemble a vagrant, but neither was he a figure of eminent respectability. Consider his shape, consider his sweat, his nerves, his manner. He would sit here and wait and steel himself for the walk home.

He missed DIY spaces. He missed the music, the tables selling zines and CDs, and the occasional cold pasta sold by eager vegans toting small coolers. This seemed as close as he came these days.

Perhaps the kids were at it, booking shows at secretive spaces around the corner, distant, the tower still looming above. But Virgil didn't feel as though he belonged to that world any more; all of his old haunts had closed or fallen out of favor. Under other circumstances, in other cities, he might have tried, might have again become a part of that community. Here, he was on the outside.

The idea to bring in quotes, some of them found audio and some of them segments he had commissioned, had occurred to Dean late one night midway through the writing of "Cornish in Mourning." He had been staring at an accidental archive that he had inadvertently accumulated during a break in his writing. He knew that some of what was on the tapes sitting in one corner of one room would be unpleasant, and yet that initial pressing of the play button was inevitable. And so a period of listening had begun.

The following day he had gone walking and had thought about all that he had listened to. But twenty minutes into it, he realized that the thing that had lodged in his brain most was less the sentiments imparted on those cassettes, but was instead the way a certain phrase had sounded. He wondered if he could chart it out, could make those words resonate against a passage of music he was composing. Only one way to find out, he thought.

He knew that he was far from the first to do this. He knew his Steve Reich and John Adams; he remembered, in his late teens, listening to an edited version of Gavin Bryars's *Jesus' Blood Never Failed Me Yet,* listening to a looped version of an old man's haggard voice breaking, again and again, thinking it was the most beautiful thing he'd ever hear. Like the punk records on which he'd thrived then, it was a way of staying alive. Sometimes Dean would cue up a certain section of Bryars's piece and listen to it again and again, half as a student and half as a penitent. He would sit and listen and jones for a particular leap. When he revisited the piece in his thirties, he was shocked at how much it had influenced his own work. Stealing from our heroes, Dean thought. It's a true thing.

Four minutes into the concert, Virgil considered learning Latin. More precisely, he wondered what it would be like to hear these pieces performed and actually understand them. Knowing the language would make them less abstract; the sounds he heard would be words with understandable meanings, rather than simply vessels for sound. He understood, on some level, that the message that they imparted was devotional. Would comprehension bring a distancing, or would it pull him in closer to the music before him? Would he have a closer understanding of the composer's intent, or would it alienate him? Or would there be some mysticism present that he hadn't previously detected; would he find new dimensions to welcome?

The music he heard now was peaceful and somber, the force of unamplified voices more than filling the church. Virgil felt a slight throb in the space between skin and bone above his ear. He rubbed it for a while, then let it phase out. At least he'd stopped sweating, he thought. He looked at the audience around him, the makeshift congregation. It had risen to over a hundred by now; the gaps around him had been filled. His pew was shared with a couple his parents' age. They sat close to the aisle, each of them rail-thin, each with grey streaks in their hair. Occasionally one would lean in close to the other and whisper something. Most of those assembled, Virgil saw, had their eyes on the singers at the front of the church. A smaller group eyed the programs: eight pages long, Xeroxed, clearly stapled by hand. Liturgical zines, Virgil thought.

The rattling tattoo rambled up again beside his ear, and then ebbed. Virgil ran his hand down the front of his shirt, his hand sketching the evaporating sweat and the spots where it could still be found. When the time came for the walk home, he thought, he might be dry.

Latin, Virgil thought. These might be demonic prayers and he'd never know. They might be descriptions of everyday life: milling grain or making ales. They could be the names of monks or a litany of offenses perceived by the composer. Virgil wondered about context. He wondered if anyone here had taken the time to understand the language that they were hearing, or all of the rest of the room was like him, perceiving the sonics without the sentiment. He assumed the singers could, but even that, he realized now, was potentially false, a bridge too far. Were they believers, he wondered, or was this simply a matter of notes for them, a sense of performance rather than passion?

Of course he was thinking about hardcore again. The music that washed over him now was dolorous and sacred. The images that filled his mind were of hall shows, of a face screaming into a guitar's pick-ups, of a figure leaping from the stage of City Gardens into the hands of a waiting crowd.

Åsa hadn't planned to be at this performance, but she'd been back in town, visiting her father to the west of here, and catching up with aspects of her life that had been dormant these last few years. An old friend of hers had had a spare ticket; intrigued, she had made her way over to the church, had wandered in. Dean up front, she thought, just like always. She thought about sending Marina a message. She wondered if she and Dean remained in touch, if what they'd had had cooled to friendship or to active dislike. Either, she thought, seemed a possibility.

And now Dean was in the middle of the composition that he enjoyed the most. It was the part that reminded him the most of being in a band. The brass surged behind him in slow crescendoes, each of which was stifled as he triggered a different vocal sample. He felt the sounds energize him, his pulse quickening now not from nerves, but from the thrill of it. He'd never been comfortable around crowds, whether twenty at a basement show or the hundreds massed here. His relationship to performance was an imperfect one. Some around him ran for the triggering of endorphins; others preferred the usage of stimulants. For Dean, it was moments like this; in interviews, he had taken to saying that the time he had spent not making music for crowds had been a particularly bleak point for that very reason.

He sent scattered voices into the audience. One was his own, taken from a live recording at an hall show eight years earlier. A bit of stage banter introducing a song, a turn of phrase that seemed like it might work in this context; in no context. Another voice was one that he had taken from a field recording, a microphone pointed out of a second-floor apartment window early one morning, hearing words shouted from a passing car window. In each instance, the brass instruments surged and then were silent, followed by the voices. These, Dean thought, were his new guitars.

Dean let the next brass part grow even more than he had the rest. The volume grew. He looked out at the people before him. He knew what the last voice would be. He had digitized it from microcassette the week before. He had used something different in rehearsals; he wasn't sure why. None of the musicians would know the voice. They would have assumptions of where it had come from, certainly, but none of them knew him. None of them would come to a sense of recognition. He hoped that this would not be self-sabotage; he hoped that this fragment, new to the musicians surrounding him, would not derail the piece. The endorphins that had sustained him fell away, replaced by a low nausea.

The key to trigger the sample sat before him. He'd come so far, he thought, and set his finger atop the button. Its matte finish was starting to wear smooth, He could reach down with another finger and prompt the sample used in rehearsals, he knew. It might be easier. He could make with the familiar here, in this space. He considered it, then opted for the original.

In her seat in the back of the church, Åsa Morgan listened to voices familiar and unfamiliar. She recognized the one of Dean easily; she'd been there, could remember the context precisely: one of the better Alphanumerics shows, albeit one where Dean's penchant for digressions when speaking between songs had reached an apex. Still, she could understand the usage of it here, even as the flood of memories took her away from the music happening a hundred feet in front of her. And then, at the end of one of the brass crescendos, she heard a phrase she'd never heard before in a voice she hadn't heard in years.

First came a cough. And then a voice, hesitant and weary. A kind of confession. "I never knew I could hate so much." Another pause. "I wish I'd never set it all in motion." And then, again, the sound of brass, much louder than it had been before.

She suddenly felt very cold. She felt the urge to sprint down the aisle, to crumple Dean Polis's shirtfront in her fist and spit the words

You have no right in his face. Instead she stood unsteadily and waited and thought of what she might say to him when they did speak. They would speak soon; of that she was certain. She had no idea of what she might say: what words, what tone. There were, she realized, many ways in which that conversation might go wrong, and only a handful in which they could go right.

There was, Virgil thought, a strange feeling in the church. According to the program, the choral program was two-thirds complete. He sat back and closed his eyes for a moment, letting the sound be the only thing that glanced through his mind. He listened to the polyphony filling the space, reverberating off the walls. It passed through the bodies around him and it passed through his own body as well. Virgil thought about this space: not necessarily designed for events such as this, but not a foreign host to them either. He tried to estimate the shape, to gauge the room's dimensions, to estimate arches and windows. He strained hard to hear sounds from outside: people walking on the sidewalks, cars passing by.

Now he was anticipating words before they came. In his mind, they registered as words. Finally they were words. They still carried no meaning, but they sufficed as words at last. He reached for them; he waited for them and craved them, craved the next one before the choir's mouths had opened.

He thought about the time to come, the time after the concert ended, when they were all dismissed from the space. Would he stand around and attempt to make conversation, or would he simply prepare his homeward trudge, then slowly step into his shower and let the caked sweat and newer sweat be cast from his body? He looked at his hand; the skin seemed far too pale. Too many days inside, he thought. Too many days hidden from the sun. He remembered riding the subway years before, of moments when he had nothing to occupy his attention. At the time, he had watched the interplay of the bones beneath his skin. Now that dance was masked. The bones seemed to have drowned.

Once more, Virgil closed his eyes. He heard the voices in song and wait for the next word to come. He began to hear patterns in the sound, and he feared that the piece might end before he could find the balance of anticipation and satisfaction. He leaned in, closer now, and opened his eyes. He heard the first sound of the word, and he knew; he saw its outline and he saw it matched and he saw its full form at last. And he knew that the word would be forever incomplete; and yet, he knew that it was complete. The word was completed to Virgil, and the word would never be complete to Virgil. The choir pronounced the first syllable of the first word in a language Virgil did not know.

It wasn't until the program had completed and the church was largely emptied that one of the event's volunteers noticed a man in his thirties, his body limp and slumped in one of the pews, seemingly asleep. The volunteer walked to the form and rustled its shoulder and slowly took in the fact that its eyes, trained towards where the choir had stood, were unblinking. The volunteer noticed the lack of breath and signaled frantically, and then began to sob.

Two years and four months and six days after the death of Virgil Carey in the town of New Dutchess, Dean Polis stood before a crowd in the city of New York for the closing measures of "Cornish in Mourning," booming and dissonant, drowning out any voices he might have summoned. Dean stood there and looked out at the audience and thought about significance. He took a deep breath and looked out at the faces of strangers. He waited; waited as the music grew louder and louder; waited as horns played in perfect harmony with one another and cellists tore at their instruments and percussionists accelerated their rhythms by subtle degrees. He looked at the audience and knew that there was something he could hide in here before the final measure, before applause, before that brief forthcoming silence. He thought of his old home, and he looked up at the sky and remembered the sight of the tower.

And Åsa Morgan watched Dean there and thought back to him as vocalist, thought back to his years making a music so different from what was happening here. And then she heard a sound she knew from years before, a sound she'd heard at countless basement shows and hall shows and in small clubs in and around the city. She looked up at the front of the room; even without the cue, she would know that sound anywhere. She knew that it would end before the rest of the music died down; she knew that applause would come, likely more enthusiastic than polite. But for now, it might have been fifteen years before; it might have been a smaller space, it might have been a sound still working out just what it would become. But for now it was, simply and subtly, the sound of Dean Polis screaming.

TWO

THE GAME OF TRAVERSAL

(1976-1981)

1

THREE DAYS INTO THE BICENTENNIAL, Carl Carey figured out the last piece of the game. His routine in those days was simple: he would drive his car to the edge of the Delaware River, where he would sit and watch as boats passed below. The boats left ripples and wakes in the water, and Carl would watch them as they faded, rippled water returning to flattened water. On an early day of this, he had thought that, perhaps, he should record that motion. On the following day, he purchased a large notepad, and he used it to chart the patterns left by the craft moving through the waters. At first, it wasn't clear why he did this. His own oblique strategy, perhaps. His own attempt to impose inspiration. He had no idea if it was working or if he'd only left himself a lunatic record, a series of scribbles that would be viewed by his family as inexorable proof of a proper decline.

The game he was working on was about evacuation. Neighbors in his old town talking about fallout shelters had inspired him even as their conversations prompted sleepless nights and startled stressful awakenings. He spent weeks reading about shelter construction and standards. He had gone to libraries in those counties that abutted the ocean to look up efficient diagrams of routes away from a flooding coastline. He had created his mechanisms to propel the game's action forward. But something was still absent, and he hoped to summon it from these idylls.

Carl Carey was a small man. "You've become a fireplug," his father had said to him one night, and since then, the description had stuck. Even now, he felt trepidation as he walked down sidewalks, that someone taller, someone more vital, might mock him for no apparent reason, perhaps in front of his children. His anxieties came in strange forms: cataclysms gave way to humiliation in front of a younger generation. Neither seemed probable to him, and yet the twitches and shudders remained.

It was an avoidance of potential mockery that had first drawn him to the car and the riverside, a sandwich wrapper usually emptied on the seat beside him by shortly after noon, a travel mug with the pattern on it beginning to fade. It was portable and private.

He called the game Traversal. Like his previous efforts, many incomplete, many in file drawers or bankers boxes in the basement, the idea had come to him in a dream. He had been on a retreat; he was at a monastery on an island surrounded by waters, entirely alone. He had, he understood, been there for a very long time. He was, perhaps, old, or ageless; there were no mirrors in which he could see his reflection. He walked through stone halls and looked at arches and saw places in which he could meditate, and the waters waited outside to receive him.

From there came notions of decisions and escape. In the same dream or an adjoining one, he dreamt of walks through a landscape that shattered under his feet. Fissures opened as he walked, a chain reaction that turned a flat surface into an array of chasms. And so began the question of how to manuever to some kind of safety even as his means of getting there betrayed him to the earth. He woke in disquiet; memories of the dream rushed into his conscious mind, and he sat upright in bed beside Marlene, let them simmer for a few minutes, and then began jotting down notes of the images that had come to him.

At first there were false starts. There always were. But in the end, the concept came to him as strangely and as simply as anything: it was about escaping from a dream.

He let it build within himself. As he discussed expenses and bills with Marlene, a part of him imagines rules and rolls of dice. As he tried to help Fiona with her algebra homework–Marlene was always the one with skills in mathematics–he kept flickering to what a game board might resemble. As he tried to teach young Virgil new words, he thought about what might constitute a turn. Over the course of six weeks, it led him to longer and longer spells of solitude. And now, he was sitting in his car overlooking the river, mulling over refinements to the game's basic concept, haunted by the sense that it was incomplete.

On these mornings, he left Virgil with his cousin. Fiona was at school and Marlene was at work. He drove through the streets of New Dutchess and saw signs of new construction everywhere. He stopped and got a cup of coffee most mornings, and then drove to the his usual spot at the overlook. He pushed his seat back so that his legs could extend with plenty of room beyond. It was more comfortable than his home office, he joked.

Marlene's cousins were his first group of testers, and he had also called in some favors, asked old friends to drive there from upstate New York and Bucks County. Sometimes he would drive out there to meet them. There were other enthusiasts that he'd met along the way, and they had also tried out different iterations of the game at different spots in the concise downtown of New Dutchess. And while he had been backslapped and urged forward and complimented on his work, something seemed off to him. Carl felt bedeviled by the element of randomness. He had set two goals for himself: to emulate the strange cascades of dream logic, and to create a game that was satisfying to play.

He needed space to think, which is how he had come to this place to begin with. The overlook and the river, and a building under construction before him. The last of these caught his attention: each day brought more and more of the building's skeleton. He didn't know entirely what it was, but he wasn't sure that it mattered. It was something created along systems and patterns. It had rules and guidelines and devices to carry its players forward. Each day's work refining the game eventually shifted into him watching the building's slow refinement. Carl watched the small shapes, barely recognizable as human, maneuvering on beams and joining objects to objects.

One cold morning he sat in the car and wrapped a blanket around his body. He had two travel mugs with him, one containing black coffee and one containing hot chocolate. His breath steamed the air before him, and he wondered how long he would last before turning on the ignition and summoning heat while the car idled, or just returning home. There had been other moments like that, when the cold had broken him. A few times, he had driven down to Lambertville and crossed the bridge into New Hope and traveled down highways until he found a diner there.

The steam he had made seemed to hang in the air before him. He was already distracted by the cold. He felt his fingertips ache and thought about seasons, realized that what was missing from his game were seasons, each with their own effect on gameplay. He leaned over to scribble out a note. From out of the corner of his eye, he saw the skeleton of the building. And then he saw a human form falling towards the earth from ten stories up.

The police called Marlene a day later. "We've found your husband." They had found him huddled in a room in Delaware. When asked how he'd come to be there, he first had no words. Then? A laugh. Then he had words. "Dice were rolled, right?" Neither as a statement nor a rhetorical question, but a genuine request made in the hopes that some authority figure would have some appropriate or accurate answer. Carl Carey was unmoored. At least he recognized it. At least he sought some means by which he might reconnect.

Carl found himself again through work. He no longer did so in his car. He draped work lights across an unfinished corner of his basement and ran long extension cords over there. There was no window. Marlene told him that it looked like a mine; sometimes she'd joke about it with him, when they again reached that level of comfort. ("Another day in the mines, Carl?" "Oh yes.") But he was productive, starting at the cracked grey paint on the wall and the yellow glow from the unfiltered bulb. Neither of his children came down there at all. The space openly frightened Virgil, and it left Fiona unsettled in her own way. She worried that one day she might see the wall reach out and pull her father in—an irrational image, she knew, but one that would dwell in her subconscious for years.

On the Bicentennial's Halloween Marlene and Carl stood by their door and dispensed candy to the handful of children who crept through the neighborhood, their bodies distorted by plastic masks and makeup. Idly he wondered about this place ten years from now, twenty, thirty. Behind him Virgil stumbled on the carpet. Carl imagined the town forward and he wondered when the building he used to watch would be done. He wondered when he would be able to look in its direction again without panic. He tried his best to focus back on the present, back on the simple tasks before him.

.   The small details of the game took longer to finalize than Carl had thought. There were more test games to be played, more groups to be recruited who weren't familiar with its earlier iterations. In the end, the blackout that took hold of the northeast in 1977 was what gave him the final element, a mechanism in the gameplay that took hold two-thirds of the way through. It was then that *Traversal* was completed, and it was then that Carl found a buyer for his game.

Carl had meetings to attend in Manhattan. For most of them he would drive to Hoboken and board the PATH, and then take that to the subway. His contacts would often advise him to take a cab: "You have the money now," they said. "Splurge." He did not. He needed the sensation of movement; he needed to look at maps of transit and understand how that transportation and connection felt as a participant.

Alternately: everything was research. Slowly he placed an underlying logic beside each of his movements after he parked his car: the payment of the fare and the entry into the PATH and the wait for the train; the conveyance from one station to the next until he reached his destination from there; his exit from one station and his trek to the subway and the repetition of the process there.

Sometimes, after his meetings, Carl would visit his lawyer. He would reverse his trip and venture home, hoping to avoid the traffic. It was its own routine, as meticulous as the timetables of the Port Authority Trans-Hudson or the Metropolitan Transportation Authority. He would arrive home and speak with the rest of his family and would sometimes head into his basement, at work on sketches towards the next project and to look out at neutral walls on which no motion could be seen.

In the midst of all of this, Carl Carey recognized his place in the middle of patterns and decided to discover the name of the man who had fallen.

This should have been simple. Surely there had been a story in the papers about such an event: a man falling from a great height, a building that would reinvigorate the community marred by a senseless tragedy. Carl had been in no condition to read the newspapers in the days after the fall, but on some level he was aware that something would have been in there. It would have had to have been. This was a quiet corner of the state; this was a place in which a burglary could be front-page news.

But Carl found nothing. He had arrived at the library a minute after their doors were unlocked; he had gone to the newspaper archives for the day of the fall and the days after the fall, and there was nothing. No news of a construction worker's untimely death or a story following up on the family he had left behind. No obituaries. He saw mentions of the nascent hotel, to be sure: local leaders excitedly extolling its vigor, its potential. But that was all. The hotel, in the story told by these stories, was not a tragic place.

Carl began to wonder if his eyes had failed him and he had seen something else. Perhaps what looked like a falling body from a distance had been a jacket, or a bag, or a set of tools. Something else to plummet, leaving only confusion, not a fatality, not grief or horror or a damaged family waiting. Carl tried to remember, and realized that his hands were shaking. He moved away from the archives and passed a silent hour in the stacks, the books around him looming like an ancient cathedral. He would not return to the library for a very long time.

Three weeks later, as he reviewed paperwork connected to the release of *Traversal*, Carl found himself scribbling a note about a new game. He pushed the paperwork to one side and drew a pad with fresh paper atop it towards him. On the paper he drew a rough sketch of a playing area. Tiers, he thought, or the appearance of tiers. He began thinking of heights and vistas. He imagined the look from his lawyer's office high on a building facing west: the expanse of New Jersey and beyond, all the way to the horizon. The way the sky would bend. The look from out of the window of a westbound airplane at twilight, the way you could see the night coming, quiet and inevitable.

Carl had grown up on the plains. He was used to long looks to either side, of expanses stretching out before him. He had never worked in a high-rise, and his time here felt confined: hills and buildings around him on all sides. Why not embrace that in this game, he thought. He thought of towers historical and mythological and religious: Eiffel to Babel and back again. He jotted ideas around the loose outline of the board: cartoon logic or genuine physics. He began wondering how he'd make it work and then drew himself back: he hadn't even begun. Still, he wondered. Could you assign points to the quality of a view? Could you make sunlight and clouds and haze variable? Could that be quantified? Would players embrace the idea of a vista that they would never see, that might well be impossible?

And then the thought of towers and heights took him to where he expected he might go. A sense of vertigo and of plunging, and then grim uncertainty. He filed away his notes and pushed those papers away. Five weeks later brought the news that work on the hotel had been halted indefinitely. Once Carl had considered mounting an investigation of the site himself. Ichor rushed to his face as he read the report. He wondered what avenues might still be open to him, even as he realized that there were none, and for that a sense of gratitude took hold.

Traversal was a success. It did not become ubiquitous in the living room cabinets of middle-class families around the country, but it sold well in the United States and various European nations. Carl and Marlene continued to live modestly. By the last months of the Carter presidency, Carl was working on his next game. This one had nothing to do with vistas or towers or anything resembling height; that project has been put inside a series of envelopes, the better to contain the panic that might arise in him if he ever gazed upon those sketches again. Periodically Carl fantasized about hiring a detective to determine what had happened; it was the lone transgression he allowed himself, an investigation that he knew would leave him ruined, whatever its findings.

Carl was volunteering more in those days. There was a library a county away where he had begun to spend time. (He had found himself unable to return to the site of his archival research–the parking spot near the river–without panic settling in and then deepening. Even now.) Mostly his work involved organization: of making spaces more optimal, of shuttling around chairs and tables. Sometimes he would spend hours in the stacks making rows of books fit evenly from shelf to shelf. It was certainly relaxing, but it also allowed him to view the world differently, as though there was an underlying order, an underlying logic. After years of sitting in a basement office and feeling the darkness and the ceiling stretch above him like an umbrella or a helmet, he felt unfit to stand for hours on end. And so he did exactly that.

Long walks in the open air helped as well. So did perambulating in circles through a somewhat familiar space. He felt as though he possessed a certain sort of access. Some hours in the library, he would walk through it when it was otherwise unoccupied, and the sensation that coursed through him was one of renewal.

It was in his capacity as a volunteer that he encountered someone who had worked on the hotel, now abandoned since that initial shutdown. It hung above the city like something unchecked, a dent in a wall that needed to be painted over but had instead festered. In other words, Carl knew that there had been no work on the hotel for the last few years by virtue of the fact that it could be seen, in its current state, from virtually any position in the town. This did not mean that he ever asked about the hotel's status, or read anything about it in the newspaper, or asked friends or family about it. It was something that he had trained himself not to see, but he had not trained himself well.

Carl reviewed the card catalogs one morning and, from behind him, heard a man's voice asking what, exactly, he was doing. He had a spiel ready for such moments. He turned and saw the man's greying beard and green jacket. The rest of him seemed largely anonymous, a few years Carl's senior. He was a face in the crowd, somewhere between anonymous and archetypal. Carl gave him the rundown: he volunteered there a few times every month, he said, and listed off his tasks for the day.

"How does one come to do that?" the man asked. Then he paused and extended his hand. "Ralph," he said. "My name's Ralph Hochetz."

Carl shook Ralph's hand. "I have some down time right now," said Ralph. "I work in construction. Next job doesn't start up for a few weeks. Life's like that." And so they got to talking, a conversation that would continue in fits and starts over the next few weeks.

Two weeks later they picked up sandwiches from New Dutchess's tiny deli and sat down at one of the town's minute parks. Ralph glanced up at the ever-present skeleton of a building. "I worked there until it all went to shit," he said. Carl's vision narrowed in on his newfound friend as though gazing at him through a long roll of cardboard. He felt suddenly forced back into this focus. It was as though he had no choice but to listen and, eventually, to respond.

"I used to come down here and park my car and work and watch it," said Carl. "So the tower would be off in the distance."

"The hotel?"

"The hotel, yes. I'm not sure I knew what it was meant to be back then."

"Well," said Ralph, "I don't know what the hell it is now. Surely not a hotel. Maybe people break in now, to squat there–though even so, I can't remember if there is anywhere to take shelter. Maybe. Might've all been open at the time we left it."

Carl felt the conversation running over its banks.

"Structure's how I think of it. 'The structure that's near the river' is what I've been saying to my family. I don't know if they like it, but we at least have a name. We've got," and here Ralph paused and fidgeted with one hand. "We've got consistency."

This was, Carl thought, not the best time to bring up the falling man. Would it ever be, he wondered? He liked this break from the routine of work and volunteer work. Bringing up what he had seen or not seen might disrupt that. Perhaps the falling man had been a friend of Ralph's. Perhaps there had conclusively been no falling man and Ralph would think less of him for his delusion. And so Carl changed the subject, righted the conversation, took it to a more familiar place. They closed out the lunch by discussing swingsets: the pouring of concrete, the best placement in a yard, how high to push one's child.

The deli's sandwiches were terrible, but the lunches persisted. Local politics were the primary subject: Ralph was aware of plans for new structures, of alterations to the town's geography, expansions and contractions, foundations and demolitions. The Careys moved to a new house; Carl hung pictures of heroes and villains on the walls of his son's bedroom. Carl allowed a new game, *Erreplika*, about finding the most faithful copy of an original object, to gestate for a while as he made the house feel like home.

A few weeks into the Reagan presidency, Ralph said that he'd be moving. "Baltimore," he told Carl. "More work down there." Carl thought, *ask*. He didn't. Ralph decamped for Baltimore and Carl watched his daughter enter high school and his son enter kingergarten. Six months after that, a postcard arrived: the first correspondence with Ralph, with details of life in Maryland. A sketch of a life, really–the basic outlines and nothing more.

"I need to ask him," Carl said to Marlene. "I need to ask him but I don't know what it'll do to me."

For a while she said nothing. She thought about it for a while and the thinking left her feeling hollowed out. She weighed the two options, the trauma that could be summoned now or the trauma prolonged, a long streak that would spread over their lives for decades. She wondered what would eat at her husband more.

"Let me look over the letter before you send it," she said. He looked at her, a question in his eyes. "I know how to interact with people," she said. Carl could hardly disagree.

Three drafts later he sent a letter off. The letter asked about Ralph's life in Baltimore and contained a few anecdotes from the Carey home. And in the last paragraph, he raised the subject. "I don't mean to raise painful memories. Once I saw a figure fall from the hotel, from the structure," Carl wrote. "Since then I've come to doubt the accuracy of what I saw. But if there is someone to mourn, I'd like to be able to mourn them." Six months passed before a response came. "There was no one to mourn," read the letter in its entirety. This marked the end of their short correspondence.

A few weeks after that, Carl began work on a new game, this titled *Unmarked Graves*. It was abandoned soon afterwards, and Carl turned his attention to sunnier things, always vowing to return to his older sketches, his models, his methods of discovery. And so the years passed.

THREE

PULP NOVELS
(LAST NOTES ON THE CITY'S TRANSIT)

(1981-1986)

1

MALLORY POLIS ARRIVED IN NEW DUTCHESS IN 1981. Though she
wore a ring and spoke of a husband in conversation, few saw that tell-
tale spouse, ostensibly named Arrington and residing on the opposite side of the globe, apparently tasked with some arcane series of
duties at a financial office in Christchurch. The visible ring, the invisible spouse, and a child: rotund Dean, a squat boy who mashed his
fingers into his mouth to gnaw at his nails and his cuticles. A cousin
of Mallory's, one Taryn Michaelson, a faculty member at a pair of
local community colleges, was enlisted to help raised the child, and
did exactly that.

Mallory had come to the northwestern part of the state for professional reasons. Put more simply: she had a legal education and a
deeper knowledge of transportation than nearly anyone else. A few
years earlier, consolidation had turned trademarks obsolete, rendered
certain lines vacant, and sparked a mode of centralization. A dozen
systems united and something new was born. Mallory's reputation
had been made as a result of a series of legal maneuverings that had
sped the transition. In certain circles, she was famous. The urban
planners in the region knew her well; she was believed in by them in
a way that few others were.

And so: New Dutchess, which wanted a rail station very badly,
which was pushing new state agencies for an expansion of rail lines
or a new rail line or something that would connect their remote
borough with Penn Station. At least, a Penn Station; they would have
preferred the one in New York, but would settle for the one in Newark.
Certain influential names in the town wanted glory, wanted to revi-
talize, wanted to create a downtown and establish something that
might draw affluence, draw spending money, draw culture. They had
very little of that; there were some old neighborhoods, but suburban
sprawl had not come in the post-war years. The town remained mostly

walkable, with a handful of businesses and a warehouse district and a couple of churches. A group of locals had amassed a certain amount of money to spark interest in the town and to, in theory, bring the railroad. Thus, the hiring of Mallory Polis, at no small salary.

***

Young Dean Polis understood certain thing as the car crossed the Delaware Water Gap and he and his mother entered New Jersey. He understood that this was a place where he could be someone new; he understood that here, his playground nickname of "Roly-Polis" might be shed. One night a few days living in their new house he turned to his mother and said, "I don't want to be husky any more." Mallory understood this, recognized some resemblance; this seemed precocious, to be sure, but it also suggested a welcome willfulness. She nodded; this was another project she could develop.

2

In March 1983, Mallory Polis met Greil Reed. This was during the heated years, the flash-flood months, the time when plans had begun to leak out to certain members of the media. The plans for the rail line; the plans for certain dreams to manifest. The trust that had hired her had assembled a slogan. They'd hired ad men on the sly and signed them into silence. The slogan was often accompanied by the arc of the projected rail line, its curvature into the northwestern corner of the state stylized and made into a proper symbol. In the logo its curve was a curtain and behind it stood a landscape: idyllic forests and welcoming shops and a panoramic view of the river.

This was how it began. Mallory sat at her desk, with a massive calendar staring back up at her from its surface. At right angles were photographs in small frames: Dean in a soccer jersey, grinning; her parents in faded Kodacolor on a family vacation in 1968; her brother on a sailboat, waving to someone in the distance. That was what she had reduced her family to. Her former husband's image was gone; images of her grandparents and a host of cousins remained in drawers at her home, but had no place here. Sometimes her colleagues would enter and look at her desk and say something like, "Stark." She would nod at them, as if to say: *anything else?* In each of these instances, she waited until they were gone and then glowered.

Still, she couldn't shake the idea that this desk was spreading in front of her like some terminal archipelago. The deep birch of the desk seemed to sprawl. If she dug under the carpet, she wondered if she might find it putting shoots into the earth. She felt surrounded by shapes: the doors leading into the office held windows like portholes, while the glass behind her felt overly vast, a kind of vulnerability. There were cork boards on either wall, and in moments when glimpsed in her peripheral vision, they seemed to quiver.

Some days, Mallory prayed for an end to symmetry.

By contrast, Greil Reed seemed to be the avatar of that symmetry. He had a crewcut that made him look like he'd stepped through a door from some branch of the military, though nothing else about his bearing suggested that he'd spent formal time in uniform. He wore shirts with clean lines; the lenses of his glasses were always spotless. Mallory imagined him traveling to sinks every quarter-hour, reaching in with soaped cloth, and meticulously drying them off. She imagined that his budget for such things must have been absurd.

For all of that, Greil's own diction was halting. He spoke in a scattershot manner, like a teenager attempting to get the hang of an older car's clutch. She first encountered this when he knocked on her office door. "Come in," she said. She often wondered why the people who'd hired her had bothered to give her an office, give her the semblance of privacy, if they were going to treat it so cavalierly. She had a preferred way to accomplish things; she studied plans and read up on legislation and made calls, the beige receiver of her phone feeling more like a bludgeon with each passing season. And so, the sound of fingertaps, and her own voice saying, "Come in," and fingers coming through the gap in the door, and then the rest of Greil emerging after the fingers had lingered for a while.

For a moment, as the fingers rested in the gap, she wondered what might happen if she kicked the door back at him; if he would yelp or if he would shriek as bones shattered. The inquiry ebbed away, and she reminded herself to warn young Dean of the dangers of such behavior, to avoid being the kicking party or the party with fractured fingers.

As Greil stepped through the door, Mallory took in the entirety of him. His demeanor abounded with uncertainty and hesitation; he looked at nearly everything in the room as though it might suddenly become a threat, from Mallory herself to the objects hanging on the walls and serving as furniture. The pallor of his skin was sickly, and his haircut gave the impression of his having settled on a style in his youth and never varying it in the ensuing twenty years. His clothing was nondescript and seemed unsuited to his build, like a raft that had partially deflated draped over some feature of the landscape. In another context, he might have been handsome, but here, he seemed simply unformed. If he was hyperaware, Mallory thought, that stopped at the surface of his skin.

He did have a reputation, though. "Greil Reed's something of a wunderkind," Mallory had heard when she'd first been hired. Could one still be a wunderkind in one's late thirties? she wondered. It was the first time she had heard the word in question, and assumed it would be the last, save for the confines of trivia games and, potentially, helping young Dean define it should he encounter it in the pages of some tome. Greil had been hired not long before she had. He saw patterns in things, and could guess at the future. He had a small isolated desk, on which she saw a large stack of *OMNI* magazines one day. He was virtually invisible in the office, and Mallory had no objections to this. One day he heard his voice raised, making the case for one computer in the office, just one, with some sort of modem attached. Weeks later she heard some kind of dreadful sound coming from that same sufficient office and assumed that it was the device he had requested.

"Bosses thought we should speak," Greil said, and took another tentative step towards her. "I'm sorry for being intrusive." Would he apologize for everything, she wondered. She answered herself: probably. Most of her colleagues, upon entering the office, would have sat by now. There were two very comfortable chairs set out right before him. Greil had not yet sat, and showed no inclination to do so. Instead he stood there beside the door like a failed hat rack.

"I thought," he said, and paused. "I thought we could schedule a meeting."

"Well all right, Greil," she said, and noticed that he shook a bit as she said his name. "What did you have in mind?"

"I don't know," he said. "Maps and timelines. Maps and plans and deadlines. Find somewhere to sit down and look them all over." Mallory wondered if this was a setup, if she was somehow being played, like something from a Jeffrey Archer novel. Was Greil here out of a genuine concern, or was this some errand on behalf of those who had hired them both, a kind of sussing out of what she was capable of?

Still. "Tomorrow," she said. "We'll find somewhere for lunch." There was nowhere suitable near New Dutchess, she knew, but there were places out there. Somewhere closer to I-80, probably, or farther down the river, near Lambertville. Or they could cross into Pennsylvania, a brief moment of exile. She hadn't crossed the state line in years.

***

Some weeks later, on one of the drives to a diner that had become their Wednesday afternoon routine, Greil began to speak about a manuscript he had written, not talking to her directly but simply speaking to the air. "It's language," he said. "Not all of these characters can be British, but if they could... A New Englander of Pilgrim stock can't use words associated with Jamestown or Jamaica. A Texan rancher shouldn't call someone a 'wanker.' It's just not done." He cleared his throat. "At least not in my circles." Mallory looked at him for a moment, but he continued to keep his eyes trained on the road ahead. "These are words I make," he said, "and lines I render." She asked him no questions on the subject of the manuscript; instead, she accelerated in the direction of their office.

3

As WAS THE CASE WITH MANY CRUCIAL CONVERSATIONS held in
the state of New Jersey, Mallory Polis and Greil Reed's first significant talk took place in a diner. In the end, they drove for over half an
hour to get there, Greil having had a bad experience in one that was
nearer to their office, and Mallory finding the food at another nearby
spot inedible. Mallory drove, with Greil in her passenger seat. Greil
struck her as the sort of person who could get lost in an open field,
who could be given precise directions and still botch his navigation,
who might eventually fold up inside himself and let the universe
devour him whole.

The diner's lunchtime crowd had begun their staggered exit by the
time they arrived. As they stood and waited to be seated, they observed
patterns in the tables' departures: a solitary diner, a trio of obvious
co-workers, a lunchtime assignation, a jovial bunch of late-career
police officers, and then back around to another soloist. Eventually,
enough parties cleared out and they sat; Greil's back faced the door.

They eyed one another, ordered immediately, and began to
converse. First came pleasantries—in this case, the anticipated mutual
recognition of one another's past accomplishments. And so they sat
and spoke of the project, the plan to birth a new rail line, or at least an
extension of one, ending in New Dutchess. The land was right. There
was the hope of money from tourism. In their office were models and
mocked-up posters and the names of prospective investors. Many
minds gestated new parks and glowing buildings and slow-burning
investments. And there was the hotel, already begun in anticipation
of the glories to come, that would look out over the river.

"Have you seen the hotel yet?" Mallory asked. She assumed he had.

Greil Reed shook his head. "No," he said. "Never had any reason
to go out by it. There's nothing to see by the time I leave work. The
silhouette's too hard to see."

"I'll drive you by it on the way back to the office," Mallory said. "It's something worth seeing.

The hotel loomed: a fence around it, and a bored security guard sitting in a hastily-built shed, reading *The Sporting News* and drinking coffee from a baby-blue thermos. They parked down the road a ways and walked towards it. From beige concrete emerged metal spindles that rose above the foundation. Even now, some showed signs of rust. The base of the building was surrounded by plywood boards, a makeshift fortress guarded from a lukewarm assault. It seemed halfway between imposing and impossibly delicate, an eggshell made, somehow, from bricks. It felt like some ancient temple, and it felt like a creature needing nurture.

No construction vehicles were in sight. Greil looked around, scanned the environs, and then turned to Mallory. "Total shutdown?" he asked, his voice hesitant.

Mallory shook her head. This is what she'd feared as they drove over. This was what people always noticed. They saw the absence of creation and they wrote the whole thing off as dead. They denoted the hotel as crumbling, and expanded that to the larger project, deemed that ludicrous as well, and went on their way. She'd had some version of this conversation before; she was certain that she would again. Mallory looked at Greil's eyes and saw some other uncertainty: an uncloaked panic, a ship-jumper's gaze. And she resolved then to bring him closer to the project, to be its most certain evangelist. "It's a temporary stoppage," she said. "Waiting on more investors." All of that was mostly true. Certain local decisions had been tabled, admittedly, and certain questions in the state's hands had become dormant. But still, there were investors somewhere. They could be courted.

She looked at the metal spindles rising out of the concrete again. For a moment they looked like nothing quite so much as fingers. This was an idea that wanted to live, she told herself. This was progress trying to get back on its feet.

Beside her, Greil cleared his throat. "Do we have access?" he asked.

"What do you mean?" said Mallory.

"Can we go inside," he said flatly. "See what it looks like inside."

Mallory had had odd requests before, but no one had ever requested a trip to see the nascent hotel's innards. She could arrange it, she assumed. It was certainly possible. Calls could be made, entry granted, hard hats distributed.

"I'll see what I can do," Mallory said.

***

Four years earlier, Greil had been living in Portland, Maine as the last vestiges of a failed marriage sloughed away from him. He'd saved some money at his last job, and was taking a break from most everything; he spent his afternoons watching the waterfront's washboard ebb and flow. He sat and he read paperback novels, first pulps and then prosperously feted works with abundant literary acclaim. The gray water before him grottoed in, gracing concrete with a wracked collision. In the intervals, he studied the prose that passed beneath his eyes and the punctual throb tapered off and then accelerated. Sometimes sibilant devotees would approach, proposing that he choose tracts from a variety of sects. Greil's hand offered punctuation and, if they persisted, a kind of warding. Greil lost himself in words—first, those printed upon the page and then, later, those that he would ballpoint in the margins. At first it seemed like a violation of some storied order, but in time it became more of a thrill. His annotations became continuations and slowly spiraled into their own tellings. His own tellings, then, inscribed on blank pages, then in journals, then in more. It continued far beyond Portland's borders.

4

IT WOULD BE ANOTHER SIX DAYS before Mallory and Greil were
granted entry to the hotel's shell. Their days were flooded with meetings and research and travels to take in prosperous rail terminals and
desiccated abandoned lines. This was what awaited if failure landed,
they heard. They walked around decommissioned lines where weeds
jutted through metal and took in that sense of squandered promise.

"This could be a city," Mallory said one day. They stood in the
middle of woodlands. Greil stared into the distance and coughed.

"It could," he said. "In another world, another now."

She shook her head. "Maybe."

Greil rubbed the hair atop his head. It looked subtly different than
it had a week earlier. Mallory wondered if he had a barber in town
that he visited and, if so, with what frequency. Mallory wondered
what, exactly, Greil did when he left the office. Her days were average: taking care of Dean, phone conversations with relatives distant
and close, and periodic dates with area men, none of them less than
fataly flawed. It was a process, she felt, that negated certain aspects
of herself. She could do without the crap roadside bars or the trips
to New York and the endless waiting in traffic. She could do without
lost reservations and wracked tensions before the Hudson had even
been crossed.

"The first job I had was down south, in the Pinelands," Greil said.
He looked at her, stock-still, hands in his pockets. "I worked in planning. There was this whole design for a city that would have been
built there, near an airport. Supersonic jets flying out of there, crossing the globe. New York to Sydney in five hours, and a city the size of
Newark a few miles away."

He coughed. "I was involved pretty late in the process, when it
was clear that this wouldn't happen. The plans were great to look at,

though. Like something science fictional. Like the ghost of a city I'd never walk through."

Mallory had certainly heard rumblings of this. She wondered how much more of Greil's life had been spent in the realm of theoretical places. It was an occupational hazard, to be sure.

"I was one of the only ones left on the project who believed in it," he said. "And so I ended up on the team that killed it, that deemed it an official folly. Circular, was how it was."

It seemed to Mallory that Greil wasn't looking for an answer or reassurance from her as much as he was seeking an audience. He might as well have told this to a security guard or made a scarecrow for the riverbanks before declaiming his employment history to the sacks and the straw.

Greil began to move, less pacing than a kind of drift, or a dance step. He went by half-measures, wounded and clamoring. "That thing where you have to unmake a city before it get made," he said to Mallory, the trees, and the sky.

Later, Mallory would ask around, and would learn that Greil's tale of his early employment had been accurate. She learned of the planned city in the southern part of their state, and that Greil had in fact worked on the late stages of it before departing for parts north.

Greil ceased his drift. He turned to her, and Mallory took this to be the start of the confessional portion of their talk. Christ, she thought, here it comes.

"I used to have dreams set in that city," he told her. He shoved his hands deeply into his pockets. "I'd be in the gardens, or the city center, or one of the outer neighborhoods. I would look around and I could see the whole thing. Most of the time I was the only one there. It was a like a prison."

Mallory had no idea what to say. While she couldn't imagine this city that had seemingly etched itself into his mind, she could easily envision him standing alone in some lost and abandoned place, in an unbuilt or unfinished city. He was waiting for something, she realized. He was waiting for input, a blinking underscore on the screen before her. Something had to be said; rather, she had to say something. Lose the words and she would lose Greil to the drift. Lose Greil to the drift and the project would be that much closer to collapse, and with it her time here. It was in this moment that she realized that she would settle here, at least until Dean was through with his education. She needed a stake in this town, and that would be it. She would tie her fortunes in with that of New Dutchess, and she would tie in those of her son as well.

And so she replied to Greil. Her instinct for the right thing to say had never been all that considerable, and she felt acutely aware of that as she began to speak. There were words forming and they sounded like pleasantries said to a casual acquaintance beset by grief–a mail-man in mourning, perhaps.

"What can you tell me about the city?" she asked. Eight words, and they seemed to deliver her failure. But, no, Greil's face was brightening. He looked at her with Christmas-morning eyes.

"I can show you," he said. "I wrote a book. Set in that city."

***

It was Tarryn Michaelson, watching Dean tap away at a plastic keyboard, his fact bowed reverently towards its tones, who heard from Dean's father Arrington. "I'm calling it a day," he told her. "Tell Mallory the appropriate monies will arrive." Tarryn, like most who knew the family, had written him off long ago, and the irreverence of this call surprised her. Like he hadn't gone already? Did he have nothing better to do than commit this final act of vanishing, to seep off strands of air in Oceania or Unalaska or Miquelon? Still, she scrawled the details of his leaving on a pad and left it for Mallory: *Absentee confirmed continued absence.* She resumed work on her lesson plans and politely presumed that some of what she prepared might, in primitive form, also apply to young Dean's education. She awaited her cousin's arrival and drew closer her materials for the cross-county drive.

5

GREIL WALKED INTO MALLORY'S OFFICE and handed her a book wrapped in newspaper. It was the morning after their conversation about potential cities in the woods. She noticed that he'd used the Sunday comics and wondered, idly, if he kept a stockpile for various gift-giving occasions. She thought better of asking that question out loud.

"This is the one," he said. "The first one, anyway. I self-published a few years ago."

Mallory began to open it, but then noticed Greil flinching, as though her tearing through the paper might also cleave his own skin.

"Can you wait?" he asked, and raised one hand in a holding gesture.

"Sure," she said, and waited for him to go. After he left she set into it, a little terrified as to what she might find. She feared the discovery of a manifesto or lunatic treatise, or something more obscure. Instead, the book she held in her hands was a very professional-looking effort. If not for the unfamiliar name on the spine and Greil's admission of self-publishing, she'd have taken it for the efforts of some towering publisher with a storied New York address. She thumbed through it and thought, good paper. On the cover, a detective leaned wearily against a building, a revolver in one hand. He looked in the direction of a modest skyline. Blue line art on a white background segued into a darker blue for the spine. The title held promise, she thought. *The Alphanumeric Murders: A David Peter Fielding Mystery.*

Mallory opened the book at random to a page. The design inside was neat, she saw. Greil, if nothing else, had that in his favor. She scanned the page and flipped through a few more: a haunted gumshoe, a missing gun, a tense chase, and abundant corruption. It felt familiar and seemed competent. She skimmed back a few dozen pages and arrived in the middle of a shootout, and read as the detective scanned the room, unwilling to draw his own weapon. She flipped back a few more, and read a short passage about kissing. A few pages ahead of that, she read a long description of a crime scene. It was there that she set down the book.

Still, she brought Greil's book back from the office that night. It took longer for her to read it in full; instead it sat in the hallway like some strange marker. It wasn't that her home was devoid of books; far from it. But they were largely shelved, often meticulously. This one stood out.

"Where'd you get this?" Tarryn asked Mallory one night.

"Co-worker's book," Mallory said. "Speaking both literally and figuratively."

"I flipped through it," Tarryn said. "It's weird. Is it science fiction? There was a chase on a moving sidewalk, and a plane that crashes on the outskirts of some city I've never heard of."

"It's an imaginary place," said Mallory. "Or a place that never happened. I don't know what the right phrasing is for that." She cleared her throat. "I'm not sure I care that much, to be honest."

"Well that's fair," said Tarryn. "Are you worried at all about Dean reading it? Might be a little violent for him."

"No," Mallory said. Still, it wasn't long before she moved *The Alphanumeric Murders* to a shelf in the office she maintained at home. It was roughly at eye level, in a space where she would remain reminded of its presence, and would in turn remember to cultivate Greil Reed and all that he might do for the project. Perhaps this pulp novel was the key to it all.

Mallory and Greil drove towards the hotel. They passed through the downtown, all chipped paint and neon and metal gone towards rust. They passed Levin's Diner and Ten Mines Bar and the bait and tackle shop that catered to a shrinking clientele of area fishermen. As they drove they passed two men with nets and tackle boxes in hand and Mallory began to say something about promise and potential and stopped short. This time they were traveling in the same car; one of the things she liked about traveling with Greil was his relative quiet when in transit.

The road to the hotel hadn't been paved in years. To Mallory, it resembled cheap special effects, the kind you'd use in some Chuck Heston disaster movie to convey the end of the world, or the world beyond that. Mallory had heard stories of this roadway devouring tires, of sections of metal jutting out to ruin trips in by maintenance crews and architects and would-be buyers of the site. As they drove over it, the car shook. To Mallory, it felt like punctuation imposed on a theoretical conversation.

They reached the shell of the hotel. The solitary security guard waved them inside and gestured to a stretch of cleared pavement that approximated a parking lot, albeit one for a much smaller building. You could fit four or five cars there at most, she thought; you could, perhaps, throw in a motorcycle if you felt like being reckless. She saw two cars, and a bike that seemed borrowed from some black-and-white television program from her childhood. As Mallory and Greil drew closer to the hotel, they noticed the air becoming stiller, and sounds drowning away. She realized that she would have to be Greil's escort here: this walk was familiar to her, and the sight of the inside of the building would not take her by surprise. She could provide a tour of this particular space.

Though the building's emptiness no longer surprised her, the lack of sounds did. One would think that sounds would come from the river, or for traffic headed there. Here there was only the wind whistling through the structure and the call of the occasional bird. Mallory noticed that Greil was a few feet ahead of her now, walking with jitters in his step, a kind of water-skier making his way over the land. She realized that Greil's mouth was moving; she realized that she could hear half-formed phrases drifting on the wind back towards her.

Greil walked through his own drift and chased it through the archway that led into the hotel's shell. She saw him stand there, the top of the arch three feet above his head. He turned back and faced her; he seemed to have become his own portrait in that moment, a vainglorious monk withdrawing into his shrine.

For a moment, Mallory recalled summers running through her old neighborhood, always in the midst of a chase. The sounds behind her, voices asking her to slow down, chiding her for safety, and the feeling of air passing over the sweat on her face. She wasn't in the habit of lagging behind, and yet, there was fucking Greil. His posture, she noted, had turned very rigid. It now appeared as though he was looking at something inside of the building. She reached him and saw a look of wonder in his eyes. "Greil," she said. "What are you looking at?"

The space looked as it had on each of Mallory's previous visits: half-made walls stood tall, and holes in the ground awaited elevators. Dirt had accrued around the empty windows. It was a ruin years before its time.

Greil turned to her and smiled. "There's so much potential in here," he said. She'd seen that look before, on the faces of young missionaries and streetcorner evangelists. For her part, she saw hazards: jutting metal and potential catastrophes on each level. There were dozens of ways to die in this enclosed space, and dozens of things that might only fracture or shatter, while leaving the wholesale life intact. At best, there was years' worth of work to be done.

Greil stepped further in. The lobby space around him was lit only by the fractions of sunlight passing through concrete and concrete and concrete, in unexpected patterns and spindled shapes. His legs seemed a half-step from sprinting. For the first time, she saw Greil restrained.

He turned back to her. "I'd pitch a tent here if I could," he said. "This is great!"

"Greil," she said. "Birds shit in here. Do you see it? Do you see the streaks? In the summer this place is a brutalist sauna. There's nothing to cherish here. Not yet."

"I know I can't actually live here," he said, still hopeful. "But a place like this. There's so much here."

Mallory shook her head. "We should keep walking. They don't like us in here too long." She knew there wasn't much to see. Ascent was not permitted, and the rest of the ground level was more of the same: a flatness, enclosed by concrete. And still, Greil's face emitted delight.

Greil took a step towards her, one arm up in some loose benediction. "All right," he said. "Let's keep walking."

***

There were no real parks in New Dutchess in those days. When Dean wanted recreation, Mallory would drive him a few towns over and sit on a bench and watch him for safe conduct. She saw him sprinting and leaping to his heart's content, a child in the process of becoming skinny. Sometimes she would see other children there—some from the towns that actually housed the parks, but oftentimes other local kids, some of whom he recognized from school and some that he might befriend in the future.

One afternoon, Dean spent half an hour swinging from bars beside a boy of the same age. His name, Mallory would soon learn, was Virgil Carey. She struck up a conversation with Virgil's father, a subtle man named Carl. She learned that the Careys lived nearby, a mile or two, bicycling distance once they'd grown older. They exchanged quiet nods, each one wondering if this might be the beginning of a friendship between their children. It didn't seem like a strange way for children to become friends.

6

TWO WEEKS AFTER THEIR TRIP TO THE HOTEL, Mallory realized
that Greil had developed a renewed dedication to their ongoing project. As she walked to her car at day's end, the sky shifting past violet,
she saw an illuminated office. The blinds were down and a sickly
orange light shone from within. That was the first time she recognized his late hours, and subsequent events and patterns reinforced
what was taking place. She heard frenetic typing as she walked past
his office on the regular; sometimes she just heard the pacifying hum
of the massive electric typewriter that dominated his desk. She would
glance into his space and see his face blank and enraptured.

Once, she jutted her head in and cleared her throat. He turned
with alarm. "Midnight oil?" she asked.

"Huh?" Greil said. "I don't understand."

So, she thought. So this. "The late nights," she said.

Greil's face already seemed disinterested. His eyes drifted back
to the paper emanating from the typewriter's roll, and moved to scattered index cards and receipts and maps, all strewn with no obvious
pattern in mind. Mallory walked off.

Stress rose throughout the office. A vote in the state's legislature
neared. This was an essential decision, though not the essential decision; not the one that had the authority to effectively close them down
and make their work irrelevant. But still, a negative vote on this
particular option would leave their office wounded, effectively broken.
A "no" vote here would be a significant tell on the ultimate decision;
much like the rest of her co-workers, Mallory dreaded that possibility.

This was Mallory's time to shine. She called in favors and made
requests. Half of her working hours were spent on the phone, hefting
the receiver and thinking of it as a sort of hammer. Briefly, she imagined a kind of combat with them used as weapons. She imagined the

office locked in battle, the floor dotted with receivers broken at odd angles and speckled with blood.

Her other hours found her on roads near New Dutchess and on roads further afield, traversing the state with strange destinations in mind. She uncovered facts and glad-handed and sussed out the town's potential futures, and sometimes idly wondered how their work might be looked on if they failed. She drove past desiccated former vacation spots and revitalized downtowns. She passed four-story glass-and-steel cubes that reflected the sun's light; she saw more skeletal towers, the hotel replicated and placed at random across the state. She saw prosperity and anxiety in equal measure. She passed towns terrified that a nearby military base might be shuttered, and she passed towns sloughing off blue laws and anticipating a lucrative bar trade.

She wondered what would happen if the rail line failed. She wondered if there might not be something to be done to salvage their work, to preserve this dream of the town. She wondered if she could manifest it somehow. But in those weeks, Mallory generally dreamt of collapse: structures falling and also floors, and solid objects rendered brittle and crystalline when they were touched.

Blessedly, Dean refrained from crying or howling at offenses perceived or imagined or tangible. He asked for little: no trips out to eat or to shop or swing on a swing. Mallory maintained a steady stream of books, some purchased from a small local shop and others procured from the town's library, a three-room building that seemed about to burst with shelves and tomes. It had been a house once, one of the librarians told Mallory; a squat building that a veteran of the Great War had called home for fifty years. After his death, a probate court determined that it had been willed to the borough, and thus, the library, previously operated from a small alcove located adjacent to the hall of records.

There was also Dean's burgeoning friendship with Virgil Carey, the first of its kind that Dean had had since they'd arrived in New Dutchess. From what Mallory saw, it was about what she had expected: two kids playing with action figures and sometimes kicking around a soccer ball. Sometimes he'd have dinner at the Carey house; sometimes she would drive the two boys to see local sights. She asked her son one night if he was happy here and he said that he was. Mallory suspected that this friendship was at the root of that sentiment.

Then there were the fragments Mallory hadn't been told when she took the job. The borough's managers had given her a short history of the town, but there was nothing unsavory in the narrative—no tales of criminals or solitude or violence or despair. Since then, she had accumulated the town's other history in fits and starts: the local drunkards who had been unexpectedly virtuous; the infamous bootleggers who had made runs up the river. The worst part about the sanctioned histories, thought Mallory, was that there was no one in them to hate. There were no bigots, no murderers, no plotters or revengers. Dig far enough, though, and you could find their leavings. She welcomed the ghosts she could fight. That was how she liked it best.

One morning, Mallory encountered Greil in their office's breakroom. Greil was stirring milk into his coffee, turning its color past caramel towards a spectral tan. He withdrew a red plastic stirrer from it. Around its base, Mallory saw accumulated sugar. Greil neatly balanced a pile of it and brought it to his mouth, then consumed it. "It's like candy," he said to her, and smiled.

"I can imagine," Mallory said.

They sat and sipped their way through their respective mugs' scalding contents. Each spoke about their current areas of focus: the calls they'd made and the insights they'd sought. They traded stories about certain rumored deals, and certain potential districts. And then Greil broached another subject.

"I've been writing another book," he said. "In the mornings, before sunrise."

Not for the first time, Mallory wondered when, precisely, Greil slept. Or if he did.

"Is this one also in the city? The one that was never built?"

"Here and there," Greil said. "The investigation covers both."

"Ah," Mallory said, and remained uncertain as to what to say next. A nod would suffice, she decided.

And then she wondered if he was a starter, if his home was full of the first ten pages of projects that were then silenced. She wondered about his own diligence and his own imagination. She had not yet formally started reading his novel. Across the table, Greil drank his absurdly sweetened coffee and sketched notes on a napkin. Mallory was unsure whether they were for work or for his novel. He looked up at her and blinked, as though he was surprised to see her there— or perhaps as though he was surprised to find himself in this office breakroom.

"David Peter Fielding is holed up in a hotel for most of it," he said. Mallory had no idea what he meant, and then remembered: David Peter Fielding was the detective Greil had made. "He spends most of his time looking at old papers and trying to figure history out from them. Have you read *The Daughter of Time*? It's like *The Daughter of Time*." Mallory had not read *The Daughter of Time*.

"It's not all moodiness and memory, though," Greil said. "A guy gets pushed out of a window. And there's a gunfight, too. Near the train station."

Mallory looked at him. "In the city where the Pine Barrens used to be?" she said.

Greil shook his head. "No. The one here." Mallory continued to stare. "Right," he said, "I should have said that before. It's not New Dutchess as it is now. It's in the town like it'll be when our work gets done."

Ah, thought Mallory. He's gone and leashed the thing we're working for to something that's already failed. And she wondered just what he truly thought of the work they were doing, or if his opinion was one of general apathy.

"There are plenty of bodies, Mallory," he said. "In the novel. I'm really happy with how it's going so far."

Mallory just nodded. Greil returned to his coffee and then, blessedly, looked back up and asked her about weekend vacations. Did she have recommendations of places that were a short drive away, he wondered. Did she have thoughts on a longer trip that might be suitable for when the difficult part of their work had ended. Mallory understood this conversation: there were rhythms into which she could fall, logical answers to logical questions. There was no sense of histories running into one another, of the city that might be over-lapping with the city that never was. That provided her some comfort as the day continued, at least.

***

The first settlement check from the distant Polis, the ill-equipped patri-arch who had failed, arrived in the mail on a crisp Saturday afternoon. Mallory looked at the not-unexpected figure on it and wondered, not for the first time, if there might be some way to dodge ethical rules and invest in the town more formally if all went well. She imagined herself as a patron. She could bend the future slightly, add a slight cant to it. This, if nothing else, she could do.

7

MALLORY FREQUENTLY TOOK WORK HOME WITH HER. Most nights she was awake until twelve or one with it. In recent weeks, as the tempo of the office became more frenetic, she was up later and later, frequently brewing coffee at ten or eleven and letting it drift through her body and call her to attention. There was a small table in a room facing the front door, and most nights it was strewn with papers and folders and index cards, there to be processed for the following day's work. On this particular night, a Wednesday, she wasn't even close to sleepy at two, and so the sound of her telephone ringing didn't come as much of a disruption. The caller identifying himself as a police officer? That gave her pause.

"We found him half an hour ago," the officer said. "The light in the window gave him away."

"I'm sorry," Mallory said. "Who is this we're talking about?"

She heard silence from the other end of the line—the hesitant sound of official confusion. In that silence, she realized who it was; there was only one person it could be.

The officer confirmed it. "Greil Reed," he said. "He asked that we call you." There were some people for whom she would accept care—at least two, that she could think of—but Greil was not one of them. And yet, what exactly was she supposed to say to the officer on the other end of the line? She assumed that he took the two of them for a couple of some sort; it was the logical assumption when an unattached man asked for an apparently unattached woman. For a brief sinking moment, she wondered if any of their co-workers had made that assumption as well. For another moment, she assumed that at least some of them did. She imagined cutting all of them, each one very slowly. Short jabs above the rib cage. Nothing severe; just something that would leave a mark.

Mallory wondered that this meant about Greil. Did he view her in some ways as an authority figure, or did he harbor some sort of desire? She assumed he was asexual; she had read a Vonnegut novel recently narrated by a man with no penchant for desire, and she had thought of Greil when she read it. But still, she had known the secretly lascivious before; if this was what Greil had in store, it wouldn't be a complete shock.

"We can release him into your custody," said the officer. "Otherwise, he's going to be here overnight. Maybe longer."

The project was in a state where Greil was essential. Greil side-lined, Greil imprisoned—that wouldn't do. She would have to get him, she realized. But as that flickered through her mind, she also realized that there was information she needed to learn. "What exactly was he doing when you picked him up?" she asked.

"The abandoned hotel," he said. "He was wandering around the ground floor when we found him." Of course, Mallory thought. Of course that was where he was. She picked him up at the police station and dropped him off at his house. Both were silent as they drove.

The next day, Mallory asked how he'd gotten in. She would regret it in time. Brodger looked inherently pidgin that morning, in a cheap button-down shirt and khakis with grease stains near the pockets. Mallory noticed a small scar near his chin that looked new. At least he was shaving, she thought.

"I timed the guard's routine," he said, "and then I ran."

She waited for him to say something more, but he kept further details to himself. There was no word on whether the security guard had made his own attempt to remove Greil or whether he had simply called the police. Greil was similarly mum on what he had seen there. It had been a clear night, Mallory recalled; against her better judg-ment, she wondered what the star-filled sky looked like from within the shell of the building, and what the nighttime light did to the space's interior.

On one hand, Mallory wanted to learn more about his night, to push him for more information. On the other, the density of their work abounded, a day full of meetings, no breaks between them. As she saw Greil in meetings, she noticed that his face seemed to be hold-ing fast to a remarkable calm, or repressing tears. In these meetings they reviewed data and updated one another on statuses, all of which was to say that they remained in a kind of limbo. She wondered how much longer that would last.

Before she left for the day, her boss, a man named Dell, called her into his office. She wondered what this meant: a confidential tip that things were headed south? It could well have been that. They sat, and then Dell cleared his throat. "So the Greil situation," he began. Ah yes, she thought, this was exactly where it was going.

"What do you make of him?" Dell asked. "Is he a liability? Are we better off without him?"

Mallory understood that, on a certain level, she had just obtained a much-needed out. She stood on the shores of something, and could easily part ways with Greil right here and now. He could be left behind, she knew. Should he be? She wondered if this was how all of his jobs ended: an awkward bond, an obsession, and then release. She thought of his maddened eyes, and she thought of enduring the scramble of the coming months without hi. Damn you, Greil, she thought. She did not want this decision to be hers; at that moment she also loathed Dell for the position in which he'd placed her.

"I can see both sides of it," she said. Dell raised an eyebrow, indicating continuation. "Losing him would hurt the system we've set up here, but he's also got problems. And I don't know what the best way to rein him in would be." She could think of no way to lure him back from the precipice. As she thought about it more, it struck her that the hotel has prompted something primal in him, something unsettling.

Mallory's gaze shifted to something behind Dell. Atop a tan cabinet, there was something still and furry. A taxidermied ermine, she saw. She found it strangely hypnotic: this dead thing atop neutral metal, its mouth open as though it was lunging for some sort of prey. But she realized something was strange about it: the pelt didn't match, not entirely. Specifically, the foreleg closest to her seemed of a different shade than the rest of the creature. Mallory wondered if the ermine was some sort of composite, a chimera made from the leavings of other corpse rodents. This was, she realized, a question she could never ask Dell.

"So we keep him on," said Dell. "Agreed?"

"Agreed," Mallory said.

"But this is it. His last chance. He plays Boy Scout once more, decides he wants another night out under the stars, and he's done."

Mallory nodded, and they exchanged brief pleasantries. As she walked back to her office, the carpet nubs beneath her feet suddenly felt like quills. She wondered whether letting Greil know of the deadline would be effective or whether Greil would be worse off knowing that he was on a deadline, that he had reached his first and last warning. Greil dealt in questions of cause and effect: she knew this from his work, she knew this from his book, all about crimes and investigations. An event took place and was resolved. As she passed Greil's desk, she saw that he wasn't in his chair. She would see him soon enough, she thought.

***

Tarryn Michaelson sat and read Greil Reed's novel. From the other room she heard the sound of Dean playing with the local kid, Virgil Carey, who'd become a somewhat regular presence in the house as of late. Something to do with action figures was happening, she assumed. This was the extent of her interest in boys of that age: they played with action figures and occasionally watched television. Neither child seemed to have much interest in sports. She was fine with that. She read through the mystery novel written by Mallory's co-worker. It wasn't half-bad, she thought. She made a note to herself to ask Mallory if he had written anything else.

8

IN THE END THERE WAS NOTHING FOR MALLORY TO DO BUT WAIT.
The same was true for the office surrounding her. The county had its
recommendations to make and New Jersey Transit had its recommendations to make. And so the office waited in a kind of stasis. They felt
like skeletons. They felt like an immovable part of something larger.
They had made their best effort and now there was nothing more
they could do.

In meetings, Mallory and her coworkers communicated in gallows
humor. They made contingency plans; they joked about hitmen
and kidnappings and sabotage. They joked about salting the earth,
though they argued about the specifics, of whose earth and how
much salt. Greil had embraced this lustily. "A wrench in their works,"
he was heard to mutter on numerous occasions. "A wrench in their
G.D. works."

It wasn't quite that they thought that their efforts would fail. It
was more that a sense of helplessness had set in. They had done everything that could be done, and now they were moving across indistinct
ground, a bridge that held no assurances that it might not collapse at
a moment's notice. And so they waited. Every time a phone rang they
wondered if it was definitive news, if it would be grounds for celebra-
tion or for a kind of horror, a preparation for a winnowing of their
ranks and a slow disintegration of their space. Mallory had an exit
plan in place about which she felt confident. Most of her colleagues
did as well. She wondered about Greil, but for all his eccentricities, he
also seemed reasonably functional. He had lived places; he had held
jobs, brushed his teeth, showered regularly. For all of his tendency to
drift, he had to have had some sort of pragmatic core.

One day she saw that someone had stapled a homemade banner
over an empty desk. "DEPARTMENT OF DIRTY TRICKS," it read.
It seemed to Mallory that the office was quieter now. Her coworkers

took longer lunches. Her coworkers also apparently had more flings, more affairs, more brief trysts. She saw it in their body language: casual touches, a hand brushing against a thigh for a moment too long.

She also saw leisure setting in. She heard one strident voice emanating from within an office with a closed door, calling in bets on jai-alai to a bookie in St. Petersburg. The young architect hired to work on a master plan was sketching baroque facades for what, she'd later learn, were a series of theoretical libraries. She assumed that Greil was using his moment in the period before the decision to find his own exit, or was jotting down essential passages for his next novel. Or both.

Greil frustrated her. With direction, Greil could be brilliant, but his manias were an obstacle. He had been quiet in recent weeks; he hadn't looked longingly in the distance of the half-made tower or talked of imagined or unmade cities. But he seemed like he might at any moment; she wondered if they might all lose him to the allure of the unfinished. On one hand, him being lost would be a horror for the whole office; on the other, so too might their project be harmed if he vanished, if he became infamous for some form of trespass.

Everyone around her needed direction, it seemed. In the case of Dean, it made sense. He was a child. He was still an incomplete project by the nature of his being a child. Tarryn, too, as she skittered across the state for various jobs and errands. Greil most of all: his work and his writing and his obsessions had spread him perilously thin. Lose that center and you might fall out of use; fall into disuse and you'd be in need of rescue. Who was Greil's rescuer, she wondered. It wasn't her. She had plenty of people to rescue already.

It was too late for her to ask Greil about matters of rescue. When they'd first met it would have been a better time, but not now. Now, she guessed, asking would only bring broken looks and distant cries. There could have been groundrules. If she could have rolled the dice again, if she could have replayed this particular game, it might have all gone differently. Something was coming. Some sort of change was on the horizon, whether positive or negative. There were only so many people she could protect.

***

Dean ran, lean and enlivened, down the track, circling it again and again. Tarryn stood near the fence and watched, her eyes more often than not glancing down at the pages of the book she held. Another lap, he thought. He'd set himself a rhythm and he'd keep to it. The beat seemed to him to be elevated above his speed. Sometimes it felt like slow motion. Sometimes he felt lulled into it, the hope that the world's unmoving tempo would fall away and reveal every movement in precise detail. He couldn't put the feeling into words, but he chased it nonetheless. He wondered sometimes if his friends felt this way. He'd ask Virgil sometime, he vowed.

As he rounded one particular corner, he caught sight of the unbuilt hotel and wondered what might be inside.

9

ON THE DAY THEY WERE SET TO HEAR ABOUT THE DECISION, Greil went missing. His car was absent from his usual spot, and there was no one at his desk. There had been no calls announcing an illness; he was simply gone. Dell noticed it and Mallory noticed it and each one grimaced at the other as they realized what this meant. Not for the first time, Mallory wondered how exactly she'd become thought of as Greil's minder. Agitated inquiries continued with the progression of the day.

At half past eleven, Mallory was called in to a small meeting. The official announcement, they were told, would come at one, but the result was defeat. There would be a catered lunch; one last positive gesture before the office went to seed. Mallory felt bleak. That would be a wake, she realized; there would be nothing left to celebrate here. Whatever New Dutchess became, it would not be the goal towards which they had all been working these last few years.

Mallory wondered what the future of New Dutchess would be like. Something more than the reality of Greil's unbuilt city in the pines but less than the dream he had of it, she realized. Her own rescue plan involved holding fast: while this plan was, as of now, sunk, there were other things to be done here, other potential futures to cultivate.

The full announcement happened at one, though the office as a whole knew what to expect from the mood of those who'd left that fateful early meeting. And so the lunchtime wake was held, and goodbyes began. Not formal goodbyes, not yet—there had been no formal layoffs made, nor an announcement of them, but they were inevitable. Instead, phone numbers were traded and hands shaken. There were no illusions here. Someone stole half the supplies from the closet where they were kept; Mallory managed a smile at this.

As she walked down the corridor past five p.m., Mallory heard a man's voice unfamiliar to her say, "Well, that's the good thing, I guess—

you never get to feel the seasons in an office, you know?" And it was true, but she regretted the smug sentiment nonetheless.

***

Mallory and Dean and Tarryn drove across a bridge from Lambertville into Pennsylvania and ate dinner that night in the town there. Tarryn asked Mallory why, and Mallory said words to the effect that it would be her last night out of the state of New Jersey for a good long while.

"But it failed," Tarryn said. "The project failed. Why not look somewhere else?"

Mallory shook her head. "Things happened, certainly," she said. "But things might still happen. There's still a future."

Tarryn wondered when Mallory had become so optimistic. For his part, Dean noted the fried potatoes before him and ingested them with joy. A little over a decade later his band would play in a hall half a mile from this restaurant, and driving through the streets, he would feel a kind of déjà vu, but he'd never quite know why. He wouldn't ask his mother if he'd been there before because those memories weren't what he took from this night. Tarryn, for her part, thought that Mallory was being ludicrous, but paid that little mind. And Mallory had other things to anticipate, and savored her meal, and made plans for the year to come and the years beyond that.

10

AS FOR GREIL, RUMORS PERSISTED. There were sightings, but nothing could quite be confirmed. Greil as vagrant, Greil as drifter, Greil as captain of industry. Mallory never asked, but still: people told her things they'd heard. They called her without prompting and volleyed out information; really, they volleyed out rumors. Some believed that he was camping in the woods by the Delaware River, or that he'd lashed together a raft and was living on a park on a small unstable island in the midst of that very body of water. Someone had heard that he had relocated to Tacoma; someone else had heard the same thing, but was certain that he now resided in Ybor City.

Three years after the rail line failed, one of Mallory's old coworkers on the project called her to tell her that he had seen an infomercial for a televangelist, and that he was sure, absolutely sure, that he was Greil Reed reborn, handling snakes and healing with the power of prayer. He was fatter and balder, but still clearly him, the former coworker said. This was the sole rumor that Mallory felt comfortable entirely writing off as bullshit.

Another year passed, and then one day Mallory received a call from the New Dutchess police. "I know this is strange," said the officer on the other line, "but you're the only point of contact we have for him." And Mallory thought, this again, and cursed.

Dean was over at his friend Virgil's, and so she had time on her hands. She drove to the shell of the hotel, which remained a shell of a hotel, a potential building more than any other kind of structure. She met the officer who had called her, a man named Ethan Chiang, and she met another detective who identified himself only as "Larson," and mostly huddled to himself, fifteen feet behind them. For the first time in many years, she walked through the doorway of the hotel and into the open space within and saw the familiar concrete walls. "We assume this is Reed's doing," said Ethan. "And we were wondering if you'd had any contact with him in the years since..."

"No," Mallory said. "None at all."

She walked through the empty space and looked at the morning light's drift across the walls. She saw the markings on them and, as she walked up to them, she realized that "markings" was the wrong word. These were words, marked on the concrete like a prisoner's record of days. These were words and they spelled out a narrative and, as she looked up, she realized that they went higher than her reach, they went higher than the reach of someone much taller, they reached heights that no one could have reached without some sort of ladder or apparatus.

Names came back to her from a novel she had been lent and which still occupied a space on her bookshelf, familiar characters but in new situations and new cities. She thought for a moment that she could explain to the officers assembled here what it was, that this was a continuation of an obsessive narrative, that she had something at home that might help to explain just what this was. Instead she looked at them and said, "Gibberish." Said, "I have no idea what any of this means." And the two detectives looked at each other and nodded.

They walked out of the unfinished hotel and left it towering and inert, words across the walls of several stories like some sort of binding spell or unwieldy manifesto. And the hotel continued to loom and periodically threatened to emerge in some new form or be demolished or simply collapse. Instead it remained as an unmade sanctuary, half-heartedly guarded, a shelter from the elements and a source of mystery and speculation for the locals. And in the many years that followed, it became a rite of passage for the daughters and sons of New Dutchess, New Jersey to break into the shell of the unfinished hotel and read the anonymous words of Greil Reed's last pulp novel.

FOUR

AN ORAL HISTORY OF THE
ALPHANUMERIC MURDERS

(1992-1999)

One: The New Dutchess Scene

THE ALPHANUMERIC MURDERS PLAYED *their first show in 1993. By the time of their breakup six years later, they had become one of the most singular hardcore bands of their day. They got their start in a remote corner of their home state of New Jersey–one which, unlike most of the state's punk scenes, lacked a recognizable sound of its own.*

Marina Ito (editor, *Plainspeak* fanzine)
This guy Bill Collier started doing shows at a VFW hall halfway between New Dutchess and Lambertville. That was the start of it, really, in the summer of 1992.

Panos "Feast" Hodges (bass, 1993-1997)
I remember that there had been some intermittent shows around us before then, in basements and backyards. But–yeah, the VFW really made things happen. It probably held around two hundred people. There were never two hundred people there, but there could be, and that meant something big. Before that, there wasn't much going on around us. You'd get a lift from someone with a car, or an older brother or an older sister. We were about an hour and change from the city, and a little more than that to Philly, and a little less than that to New Brunswick. City Gardens in Trenton was closer.

Diane Ost (drums)
City Gardens shows were always fun, except if you got lost in Trenton afterwards. Which happened a lot.

Panos "Feast" Hodges
I remember six of us in a 1985 Chrysler Laser, driving down the highway. That happened a couple of times, and you'd usually have to decide if you were going to try to squeeze three or four people in the back seat, or totally illegally wedge someone in the hatchback. It would

depend on how skinny everyone was. I was never a skinny guy. My friend Virgil, same. So if we were in the back, someone was laying on top or someone was rolling the dice in the hatchback.

Marina Ito
The fact that there was an all-ages space close by meant so much to us.

Emmett Foster (guitar, 1994)
Bill Collier was impossible to read. Good friend of mine, though. He would tell me that, once he'd gotten the word out, he would get plenty of calls, of bands coming through. Mostly northeastern bands, though every once in a while he'd hear from a band touring from California or Canada.

Marina Ito
Every once in a while you'd hear about a basement show close by. Maybe in Morris County, or maybe further south. We didn't really get further south than Middlesex County in those days. There were certainly things happening down there, but–word never reached us, really. You'd hear something about a hall show in Highlands or see a photo in someone's zine and think, "Wait, that looks like that basement I was in that one time." And then you realized that you'd retroactively missed some band's entire tour.

Panos "Feast" Hodges
I remember wishing that there would be a good record store some-where near us. We did a lot of mail order back then. Send a check to California, wait for it to clear, wait for something to come back via media mail. It was awesome. You can tell that I'm being sarcastic here, I hope. I really want to make sure that my sarcasm is properly captured, that your readers don't think I'm some kind of masochist for youth crew records.

TWO: EARLY SHOWS

The Alphanumeric Murders began playing together in 1993, and booked their first show for early the following year. It was a hall show set up by Bill Collier: they played first out of five bands. The Columbus, Ohio band Treestump would headline.

Everett Wilhelm (vocalist, Treestump)
We were touring in early 1994. We'd had a show in Wilkes-Barre the night before, and we followed it up with this hall show somewhere in north Jersey. We'd had a flat tire on the van on the way out, so we got there a little late, and only got to see a few songs from the first band. It was pretty good! We hadn't realized then that it was their first show, so that was even better. It's funny, too—running into Dean [Polis] a few years later and realizing that that had been where we first met.

Panos "Feast" Hodges
I remember being in the same study hall as Dean Polis when we were juniors in high school. That was how we first met. My friend Virgil—also his friend Virgil—introduced us.

Diane Ost
There was this guy Rollie Sturges on drums when they were starting out. He and I used to skate together, weirdly enough.

Julia Wittimer (guitar, 1993-1995)
I don't even know what to say about my time in the band.

Diane Ost
No one's heard from Rollie in years. I don't enjoy thinking about what that means.

Julia Wittimer
I'm sure everyone says that they were a different person at that time in their lives. I know I certainly was.

Diane Ost

Rollie was a nice kid. "Kid." He was a couple of years older than the rest of the band–Fest and Julia and Dean. But the last time I saw him he was twenty, maybe? So yeah, "kid." Him then still feels older than me now, though.

Julia Wittimer

I heard that these two guys who were a year younger than me were starting a band and needed a guitarist. That was cool. There weren't a lot of people in our high school who listened to anything abrasive. There were a couple of guys who liked metal, but they were creeps. I've met plenty of people who liked metal since then who weren't creeps, but these guys? Total fucking creeps.

Diane Ost

Rollie and I would be out skating near the river and I'd hear about how things were going. I knew Fest, and I knew Dean pretty well. My sister Alanna was into a lot of Dischord Records stuff: Rites of Spring and Embrace and Dag Nasty. I went to a few shows with her when I was twelve or thirteen, before she went to college. I remember being terrified at first. And then I wasn't terrified any more.

Panos "Feast" Hodges

I remember Dean knew Rollie and I knew Julia. It was a pretty easy time, getting that first lineup together. We practiced in Dean's mom's basement a few times a few times a week, and things came together pretty well.

Diane Ost

Rollie played me a song from their practice tape. It didn't suck.

Panos "Feast" Hodges

I remember really wanting to do weird things with my bass. Maybe things that, in retrospect, couldn't be done with a bass. At least not with the bass setup I had.

Diane Ost
Dean had a pretty good voice. He could sing, and he could scream so well it made your throat hurt if you tried to sing along.

Julia Wittimer
Our first show–do you mean the first show in an actual space, or the time we played four songs for some friend's in Dean's mother's basement? Because that was pretty fun. The first time we played in an actual space, I puked. I puked before the show and I puked after the show. So did Dean. So did Rollie.

Panos "Feast" Hodges
I remember I didn't puke at our first show.

Marina Ito
The first show? Dean bleached his hair blonde for it. Julia had these giant overalls on. Rollie decided he was going to grow a beard and it looked terrible. And Fest looked completely normal, like he'd run over there from a job at the mall or something.

Diane Ost
There were five of us on the bill, and maybe seventy people showed up. There was a guy in the corner selling cold vegan pasta, with olive oil and salt and pepper. That was essential. That was my dinner at so many punk shows over a couple of years. I really want to find out sometime that one of those guys ran with the idea, that they have some kind of chic restaurant in LA and it all started with them selling cold vegan pasta out of a cooler.

Marina Ito
It was their first show, so they went on first. They had a different name back then. They didn't become The Alphanumeric Murders until the third show, maybe.

Diane Ost
I have no idea where the name came from.

Panos "Feast" Hodges
I remember it was Dean's idea.

Diane Ost
I meant to ask my friend Virgil a couple of times. He and Dean were close for a long while, and I figured that if anyone knew about it, it would have been him. By the time I thought to do it, he and I had fallen out of touch, and by the time I figured out how to get in touch with him, he was gone.

Julia Wittimer
We had seven songs of our own ready for the first show, and we did a Soulside cover early on, too. The Soulside cover was leagues better than any of our own songs, and we made a huge mistake by opening with it at our second show. Admittedly, it was the best song we knew how to play. But there was a big vocal change in it, and Dean would always treat it like a dare, to get his scream big enough to fill the room.

Marina Ito
Dean's voice was always fucked after they did the Soulside cover. If they played it last, it just meant that he'd cough a lot when he talked to you. If they did it first?

Panos "Feast" Hodges
I remember being amazed that we made it to a third show.

Diane Ost
At the second show, Dean's voice sounded way beyond dirty. It sounded diseased. Which was great.

Julia Wittimer
We did our best to make it through the set. We barreled through it. I broke a string on the fourth song and just kept going. I broke another string a few songs later. We kept going. Me changing strings, having to tune—that wouldn't ended anything resembling momentum that we had. It was the fastest limp we could do.

Three: Making a Demo

The band decided to record a demo not long after changing their name to The Alphanumeric Murders. It was a time-honored tradition, but one which didn't work out terribly well for the quartet.

Panos "Feast" Hodges

I remember, out of our first crop of songs, maybe one of them made it to our first seven inch. Most of them were on our first demo, though.

Diane Ost

I'd rather not talk about the demo.

Panos "Feast" Hodges

I remember going into the studio to do the demo maybe seven months into our time as a band. We knew a guy at William Paterson [University] who had access to a studio who offered to do it.

Julia Wittimer

I mean, it isn't awful. I have worse demos at home. Some of them might not be playable. Certainly, I haven't gone back and checked. Nostalgia only gets you so far.

Diane Ost

The bass is the loudest instrument on the demo. We were not a funk band, and yet.

Julia Wittimer

We stopped by the studio in pieces, based around our schedules. Classes and jobs, for those of us who had jobs outside of school.

Diane Ost

I played it for a friend who said that it sounded like music made by a bunch of people who weren't in the same room when it was being made. Which was 100% accurate.

Panos "Feast" Hodges
I remember Dean was the only one who was in the studio for the majority of the recordings.

Diane Ost
A lot of bands would sell their demos. There was never really any talk of us doing that. We printed up some shirts and patches, sure, but–that was it.

Julia Wittimer
If some label ever came to us and asked about doing a rarities compilation, I don't think the demo would be on there. We didn't make too many copies, and thankfully, no one's ever worked up the energy to digitize it. Wait, you don't have it digitized, do you? No? That's a relief.

FOUR: AND THEN THERE WERE FIVE (BRIEFLY)

Soon enough the band was changing, with the addition of a fifth member. Not long afterwards, the band made plans to record their first seven inch.

Emmet Foster
Dean asked me to join the band around August. Mostly on acoustic guitar, at first. He said that he liked the balance of sound, whatever the hell that means.

Julia Wittimer
It didn't sit too well with the rest of us, to be honest. We all liked Emmet, but the acoustic guitar sounded weird . It wasn't the right dynamic–at least, it wasn't the right dynamic based on where we were as a band around then.

Diane Ost
At the time, we were still a pretty straightforward hardcore band. Dean had the idea to go more melodic, hence: Emmet.

Julia Wittimer
Dean had this genius plan, and then went to college. Which wasn't a long trip, but still.

Diane Ost
He was commuting from his mom's house to Ewing most days. So, forty-five minutes there and forty-five minutes back, maybe? It seemed to work out all right for him.

Panos "Feast" Hodges
I remember a couple of us were taking classes at the community college. I was going to Montclair State, which wasn't a bad drive for me.

Diane Ost
We were still writing songs at a pretty good clip. I think Emmet being in the band made things more tense, but we were working it out in the music. We decided to record something more than the demo, and we were idiots and didn't realize that there was, as you know, a really great studio right under our noses. So we asked around.

Panos "Feast" Hodges
I remember we played a couple of shows with a band from western Pennsylvania called Dragstrip. Pretty straightforward pop-punk. They had two songs about farting, and one song about setting lawns on fire. I'm pretty sure their drummer is a cop now, which is even funnier.

Julia Wittimer
Our friend Ciril was running a label. We used to see him when we'd go to Trenton for shows at City Gardens. He said one day that he'd be up to do a seven inch.

Emmett Foster
There was a studio near Lambertville that the guys from Dragstrip recommended. So we practiced the hell out of five songs and went in. It was us and the occasional significant other and the occasional friend of the band. This guy Virgil who was close with Dean and Diane came in a few times and nodded his head a lot.

Julia Wittimer
We did four songs for the seven inch, and one more for a compilation on a small label in Washington State.

Panos "Feast" Hodges
I remember Dean had a terrible idea for the title.

Diane Ost
Oh God, the title. Something like *The Mystery Begins*. The cheesiest thing imaginable.

Emmett Foster
He had this whole plan that our inevitable last record could be called *Mystery Solved*. Dean had a good sense of long-term planning even then, but his actual sense of execution wasn't great.

Panos "Feast" Hodges
I remember we all settled on having it be self-titled.

Diane Ost
I think it sounded fine. My drums don't sound good, but that's because I wasn't a very good drummer back then. No fault of the recording.

Panos "Feast" Hodges
I remember really liking it when I first heard it. Now, I'm less taken with it, but still, it's good. I think the version of "Ancient Weapons" we did on *Made Machine* is better. But it's a good first record.

Diane Ost
Dean spent a lot of time in the studio for the mix. Probably more than any of us. I don't know if that was an educational thing for him or something to do with his vocals taking less time to record than any of the instrumental parts.

Julia Wittimer
I don't really know how he balanced it all. Recording and mixing and being in college full-time.

Diane Ost
I was never a big fan of the acoustic guitar/electric guitar combo, but it did sound pretty good on that record. "Found Photos" and "Goner Cinema" still sound really interesting to me. I've gotten pretty jaded, but those two songs work well.

Panos "Feast" Hodges
I remember realizing a couple of years ago that I was the only person in the band that Emmett still talked to. And I understand why.

Emmett Foster

I quit the band not long after the record was recorded. Something about how the guitar sounded on it didn't sit well with me, like Dean had fucked with the sound of it. I just couldn't get into that. If we're a band, we're a band–that guy doesn't get to override things just because he feels like it. If he'd asked, it would be another thing entirely. But he didn't. So fuck him.

FIVE: PLAYING NEW YORK CITY

The Alphanumeric Murders played their first show outside of New Jersey in mid-1994.

Marina Ito
One night Dean told me that they'd be playing a matinee at ABC No Rio. He was ecstatic about it. We'd gone there the year before to see Merel play. It was no one's idea of the best place to see a show, and it was also an incredible place to see a show.

Panos "Feast" Hodges
I remember being first on the bill. Which was great, since the rest of the lineup was a lot better than we were. There were these two bands from California that were touring together: one of them, Slynx, had some absolutely beautiful guitar parts with terrifying vocals over them. The other, Astroville, played these fast, loud songs—they were all around forty-five seconds long.

Diane Ost
Their drumming made my teeth shake. It was great.

Julia Wittimer
The Alphanumerics ended up doing a short tour with Astroville a couple of years later. This was after I'd left the band. Dean and Diane were pretty amused about that.

Diane Ost
Astroville had gotten even more nerve-wracking on stage in the intervening years. In person, they were incredibly nice. If I didn't know them, though, I'd be terrified.

Panos "Feast" Hodges
I remember it was a brutally hot day. The space was crowded. Even going on first to a group of people who were mostly indifferent

towards us, we were sweating out small bodies of water. Dean took his shirt off two songs in.

Diane Ost
Pretty much everyone had their shirts off at that show.

Julia Wittimer
Being a punk band in the 90s meant you didn't see much air conditioning.

Diane Ost
I hate air conditioning. Don't believe in the stuff.

Panos "Feast" Hodges
I remember Dean kept talking about going back to being a five-piece. He had some people in mind, and I had some people in mind.

Diane Ost
My younger brother had basically been to every one of our shows at that point. There was talk of him joining in. It didn't hurt that he was a really talented guitarist, nor did it hurt that he had never gone through a classic rock phase like the rest of us. But then he started his own band instead. That was probably for the best for everyone involved.

Six: Making an Album

At the pace that the band was writing songs, it soon became clear that it was time to head back into the studio. Initially the band considered doing another demo or possibly a seven inch, but opted instead for the plan of recording their full-length debut.

Diane Ost
We booked studio time for around Thanksgiving to record the album. We figured we could do fifteen songs in three days, which turned out to be a terrible idea.

Panos "Feast" Hodges
I remember we were pretty rushed when we did it. In retrospect, I think the album sounds pretty good. I mean, half the records I loved then and love now were the ones that came out on SST in the 80s and were recorded in a day and sound terrible. The songs are still great, though. So if you were going to ask, I'd say that we did it in the spirit of those records, even if we totally didn't do it in the spirit of those records.

Julia Wittimer
Dean was a mess that fall. He kept saying that the semester was going well for him, and maybe it was. But we were also working on booking a quick tour for January–Buffalo and Cleveland and Pittsburgh and maybe Wilkes-Barre–and it always seemed like he had things on his mind. He was stressing out trying to get his lyrics finalized. Not all of the songs were done by the time we stepped into the studio; I think we pretty much wrote "Plankton" in there. And somewhere in all of that, he and Marina started making out.

Marina Ito
Dean and I were hanging out and talking a lot in those days. Mostly

about the band. We'd tape seven inches and swap them. That kind of thing.

Panos "Feast" Hodges

I remember wishing I knew the word for when you slowly realized that two of your friends are hooking up, and have been hooking up for a while, and you've been completely oblivious to it. I talked to Virgil about it once. We compared notes, to see which of us had figured it out first.

Marina Ito

One night he said he'd been into me for a while and I asked him if he'd written "Levelers" about me. His face got really red and I started laughing. Then he started laughing. And then I kissed him.

Panos "Feast" Hodges

I remember thinking that their relationship was something I had to protect. I'd introduced them, so I had a stake in it.

Marina Ito

We were a secret couple for a little while, and then we dropped the secret. You remember. It was nice.

Diane Ost

For the album, we went back to the same studio where we did the seven inch. Was it a perfect choice? No.

Julia Wittimer

Dean wanted us to track some acoustic guitar onto the songs. Even then, I think he wanted to go back to a two-guitar setup. We were all pretty good with how things sounded as they were.

Panos "Feast" Hodges

I remember being absolutely exhausted. I don't remember parts of the third day. Blurs, is all. I stood in the studio and drank a bottle of Jolt. You remember that? Had twice the caffeine of regular soda? I drank a liter of it. I think I still have the shakes.

Julia Wittimer

In the end, Dean didn't have time to do the second set of guitar parts. I'm still not sure who he thought was going to do them. Me or him, maybe. We hadn't met Marco yet.

Panos "Feast" Hodges

I remember finishing the mixes was exhausting. I didn't have any distance from it at the time, and I just wanted to rethink everything I'd played. And our songs weren't that complex yet, so in retrospect that seems ridiculous.

Julia Wittimer

I was thrilled when we were done. I might have threatened to punch someone. Panos, I think.

Panos "Feast" Hodges

I remember Julia threatening to stab me, and being terrified. I think I tried to hit Dean. This was deep in my Jolt fugue.

Diane Ost

Is Panos talking about fighting people again? He wasn't. That was Dean's jacket. He'd slung it over a bass. Panos was on so little sleep and the light in the studio was terrible, and he sort of...stumbled past it.

Panos "Feast" Hodges

I remember apologizing to Dean for a month after that. I had these squat feelings in the pit of my stomach for weeks at a time. I was glad he was cool about it.

Julia Wittimer

In the end, we were all pretty happy with the album. I wish the drums sounded better, though.

Diane Ost

I feel like the Alphanumerics' music has aged pretty well. I'm incredibly proud of that. But the drumming on all but three songs of our entire discography makes me cringe.

Seven: Talking With Labels
Once the album had been recorded, the question then arose: what to do with it? The answer eventually came through a band they'd done a few weekend tours with.

Arno Fields (owner, Hovercraft Music)
The Alphanumeric Murders did a couple of short tours with a band called Reworkings, who we'd worked with. Their singer, a guy named Sam Nevers, wrote to me and had good things to say about them.

Diane Ost
We really had our fingers crossed. Hovercraft had released a lot of records we'd liked. And Reworkings had told us that they were good people to work with.

Arno Fields
I was pretty excited. But then there was the whole "we're losing our guitarist" thing, which worried me.

Eight: Lineup Changes Continue

The Alphanumeric Murders seemed to be on an upward trajectory, with independent label interest, an increasingly-compelling live show, and the recording of their debut album. Things were complicated when founding member Julia Wittimer announced that she was leaving the band in 1995.

Julia Wittimer
I'd been playing in a trio for the last year or so I played with the Alphanumerics. Starting out, the name of it was Arsnarl, and then we realized that was too much of an inside joke, and we changed it to Annotations. I liked Annotations a lot better. Six months in, we started playing shows. It's funny. You never really get a sense of how big your band is, or how big your friends' bands are, when you're in the middle of it. But I did a little bit when I'd see our name on flyers. You know: "Annotations (members of The Alphanumeric Murders)." Or, later, "Annotations (ex-Alphanumeric Murders)." That second one lasted for a while.

Diane Ost
Julia had mentioned to me that she was thinking about quitting the band. I knew some people who could be in five bands at once, but I still don't know how they did it. She'd been playing in multiple bands, each of which was playing a lot of shows on the regular. And she was going to college. So–I think everyone knew that her leaving the group was inevitable.

Panos "Feast" Hodges
I remember Annotations being really, really fucking good. They were a lot better than us, to be honest.

Diane Ost
It's funny, because–they ended up being a band for a lot longer than we were. They did the "indefinite hiatus" thing before it was cool. So when they finally did do a reunion, it felt that much more organic.

Julia Wittimer
I told the rest of the band that I'd be leaving after the summer. I wanted my leaving to be amicable, and I wanted there to be plenty of time for a new person to get up to speed. The experience with Emmett had everyone a little reluctant to be too contentious with a new person, you know? We knew a lot of bands that had had people coming and going, and we wanted to keep the drama at a minimum. We didn't want scene drama.

Panos "Feast" Hodges
I remember we announced it at a big show at an all-ages space in Lambertville. It was a bittersweet thing. Julia had written a lot of those songs. She had a really distinctive guitar sound, and we weren't really sure how we'd keep that up without her.

Diane Ost
That's always the question, right? Do you want to try to find someone's Mark II, or do you take the leap and hope people come along with you? We had a record recorded that we were pretty sure was going to come out, we were planning on doing a lot of touring, and there was definitely a concern that this might kill the band. There are so many lost records like that, where a band made something fantastic and then fell apart afterwards.

Panos "Feast" Hodges
I remember hanging out with Dean and talking a lot—a lot—about who would replace Julia. Who could replace Julia. So finding Curt was serendipitous, to say the least.

Marina Ito
I'd met Curt Allston at the first punk show I ever went to. He looked aggressively normal. Almost goth, but not. He was this monochromatically pale guy. Everyone seemed scared of him, so I was intrigued.

Curt Allston (guitar, 1995-1997)
It was weird. I liked hardcore, but I never had much affinity for playing it. Which is funny, considering where Dean ended up going, and

where I did. Verse-chorus-verse, breakdown, mosh part: that was my life for a few years after the Alphanumerics ended. I don't know where it would have gone from there. One chord and the drummer kicks over the bass drum and that's that?

Julia Wittimer

We did a couple of practices together, which was nice. The funny thing is, we hit it off really well, as humans and as musicians. We kept kicking around the idea of a side project, jamming and seeing where it went, maybe bringing in some other people. We never did. Who knows, though. Maybe we still might. We're both still playing out: I see him every six or eight weeks around Jersey. He has kids, so it's not as much at shows, but still. Sometimes I see him at Home Depot, buying lumber or doorknobs. It's a weird life.

Curt Allston

That was always the thing in those early practices: trying to see how much I could make it my own without fucking it up. And there was Dean, watching it all happen.

Diane Ost

I think when Curt joined the band was when Dean's relationship to the music really started changing. He had some interesting melodic ideas, so there was always some good give-and-take with him.

Panos "Feast" Hodges

I remember he definitely had a way he wanted things to be. Sometimes we could pull that off. Sometimes not. It wasn't dictatorial, though; it wasn't like that. He would ask for advice a lot; he was always trying to push himself into weird places. Diane figured out some vocal things he could do that really differentiated him from other vocalists. I mean, it was mid-90s hardcore: you could scream, you could bark, you could sing, or you could do this kind of accentuated talking. We broke it down and we figured out a way that Dean's vocals could do something a little different.

Diane Ost
It was a strange time. You followed bands long enough, you knew about members leaving and members coming in. It was weird for us when we we realized that, yeah, what the band meant to us at that point in 1995 wasn't what it meant to us when we started it.

Nine: Label Problems

Drama continued to surround the band and their newfound label, with the group's fluctuating lineup making things even more confusing. They ended up resolving their issues by venturing back into the studio, adopting a more spontaneous approach that would serve them well going forward as a band.

Arno Fields
At the time, we were still flying by the proverbial seat of our pants. We were eager to work with the Alphanumerics, but their guitarist quitting gave us some pause. Things like that had happened to us before: someone quits and suddenly it's the end of the band. Not to sound crass, but: we wanted to wait and see if this was the kind of lineup change the band could weather. And by "we," I mean me. The label was always a pretty small operation.

Diane Ost
The guy from Hovercraft was basically dicking us around. I could see where he was coming from, but still. But we'd been through this before—it wasn't the first time someone had left the band, and it wouldn't be the last.

Curt Allston
I knew a guy at William Paterson [University] who had access to a studio there.

Enoch Etzen (recording engineer)
I had all of a day and a half. So they came in. I got to record their first song with Curt, which was a huge thing for me.

Diane Ost
We figured, if nothing else, we had a song for a compilation. We had some options there.

Panos "Feast" Hodges
I remember we only ever recorded the one thing with Enoch.

Enoch Etzen
I've been living in Montana for the last ten years or so. I teach out here; I take in rescue cats. It's not a bad life at all.

Panos "Feast" Hodges
I remember being bummed we didn't work together again, because I love how my bass sounds on that recording. It never sounded that good before. It wouldn't on anything else we did afterwards.

Diane Ost
The song was called "Bowie," and I still don't know why. I've parsed the lyrics a lot over the years, and I can't figure out what it has to do with the singer or the knife. But hey, it's a good song. Maybe the best imagery Dean ever came up with.

Marina Ito
Dean had taken a vacation with his mother to visit his great-aunt in upstate New York, he told me. They were taking the train along the Hudson, and he had this sighting of something after she'd fallen asleep. He told me—I want to make sure that I remember this correctly—that he was in the river valley and was in a canyon at the same time. He was reading words moving along the side of the canyon, and those words were what he was trying to get at when he wrote the lyrics for the song.

Panos "Feast" Hodges
I remember that one always being fun to play. It baffled people when we did, though. You couldn't sing along to it. You couldn't mosh to it.

Curt Allston
The vocals in it are done in a really strange way, too, like some sort of counterpoint to the melody. Some Meredith Monk shit.

Diane Ost
Someone asked me a while ago where Dean's shift into composing began. I'm going to go with "Bowie." I think that's fair.

Arno Fields
I liked it. I wasn't sure what to expect, but I liked it a whole lot. So we ended up with a deal.

Ten: The City, Revisited

One of the band's first shows with Allston in the lineup found them returning to ABC No Rio. And while it was ostensibly a return, many of those who were there noted that the group was playing with a newfound confidence.

Marina Ito
I thought Curt was going to keel over at that show. He basically sweated out a whole person.

Curt Allston
Our van was pretty much ruined by then. We hadn't gotten it fixed yet, so all our stuff was divided between three cars. Carrying our gear in was kind of a nightmare.

Panos "Feast" Hodges
I remember we were playing with a band from Birmingham called Ports of Call. The Birmingham in Alabama, not the one in England. They were pretty great. We'd run into them on the road every once in a while.

Pat Robataille (vocalist, Ports of Call)
The Alphanumeric Murders were always a fun band to see live. That was the first time we actually played with them. It was strange and dissonant; these long drony parts that would just explode outward. They were still a hardcore band, but they were turning into a really weird one.

Curt Allston
I thought it was fucking great. It was incredibly loud. My ears rang for days afterwards. Plaster was falling on my face for half the set. I could barely see, there was sweat in my eyes the whole time. To this day, I think it's one of the best shows I've ever played, in any musical context.

Marina Ito

It was something. Dean had started to figure out how to be on a stage, or at least he'd started to think about it. So for half the songs, he'd be totally aloof, and for half of them he'd be completely in people's faces. It was uncomfortable. He certainly made people uncomfortable, and I think sometimes the physicality of it made him uncomfortable.

Panos "Feast" Hodges

I remember thinking that I'd definitely be scared of Dean if I didn't know Dean. He was so, so intense. It was a weird kind of intense, but still. And, I mean, we'd gotten into this music because we liked weird stuff. So it made sense. I think.

Diane Ost

That show still stands as one of the high points of my time in the band. We played there once more, one of the last shows we did. But to know that I'd played a show there, and that it had been that good–that felt really satisfying. I felt a big connection to that space, to what it stood for. I don't know if Dean did as much. We certainly had similar ethics, but he always seemed a little more detached. It was something that never really came up, even though we talked about nearly every other subject imaginable during our time in the band. It's more of the retrospective effect. Things make a different kind of sense when you're looking at them after the fact.

Eleven: Finalizing the Album

With the relationship with their label solidified, the band began to finalize the album, settling on artwork and changing the track listing slightly due to feedback from the label.

Marina Ito
Dean knew a few good photographers, so the artwork side of things was pretty well settled.

Diane Ost
There was some discussion of maybe trying to have old-school liner notes, like on a jazz record, on the album. I think you would have been the person we'd have asked for that, if it had come to it. But in the end, we figured that was a little too ambitious.

Curt Allston
The guy from Hovercraft made the suggestion of putting "Plankton" first, which I think was the right call. "Plankton," "Forbes Oh-Five," "Scaffold," and then "Monsters of the Deep"–that was a really great way to start things off.

Diane Ost
We tried to get Dean not to do the radio play.

Panos "Feast" Hodges
I remember really liking the idea of the radio play. Years later I bought a Les Savy Fav singles collection and they did a radio play. Why not us?

Curt Allston
You know how, on the reissue, "Grizzlies" got cut? I like to view it as evidence that Dean has grown wiser with age.

Diane Ost

Somewhere, there's a parallel universe where Dean's a great radio producer. But it's not this one. I don't know why he thought a three-minute thing about a bear attack was a good idea, but it wasn't. It wasn't then and it isn't now.

Panos "Feast" Hodges

I remember not have any idea what Dean was thinking. I still don't.

Curt Allston

Every review that record got in, like, every zine, had a "This record is great, except..." That "except" was always the same thing.

Diane Ost

I think that really terrible decision made the record click with people, though. Like if [My Bloody Valentine's album] *Loveless* had a big ol' fart right in the middle of it. People would still love it, but they'd also have something to talk about.

Curt Allston

The songs themselves sound great. Well, they sound good. Though the guy recording it couldn't record drums worth a damn. Not like that was a problem specific to us, or to that record.

Diane Ost

Eleven songs all in all, plus "Grizzlies." It had some guitar, but I'm not going to call it a song. One of the few risks Dean Polis ever took where he ended up falling flat on his face.

Panos "Feast" Hodges

I remember we decided that the album should be self-titled. On that we were unanimous.

Diane Ost

It was a good fall. We played most weekends. We got out to Wilkes-Barre, we played our first show in Philadelphia. It started getting colder. We settled on the cover art, and the label started sending ads to zines.

Panos "Feast" Hodges
I remember we played most everywhere. VFW halls and a regional library and community college lunch rooms.

Diane Ost
And we were writing songs at a really good clip. Curt being there really sparked something.

Twelve: Serious Touring

Up until that point, the Alphanumeric Murders had largely embarked on short tours. With an album due out, though, it seemed like the time to make much more of a serious go at it—both in terms of the regularity with which they'd be on the road and the distances covered.

Marina Ito
It seemed pretty apparent to Dean—to everyone in the band, really—that they were going to be on the road for a lot of 1996. Most everyone was in college then, so the plan was basically for a short tour in the spring, around the time that the record came out, and then a lot more in the summer.

Panos "Feast" Hodges
I remember, we were going to figure out where things stood after the summer tour.

Diane Ost
A lot of our weekends were spent touring. Boston, a lot. We almost played a fest in Baltimore, but it fell through, by which I mean that we fell through. It was a big juggling act. Metaphorically speaking, though we did play with a band from out west whose singer was an actual juggler.

Curt Allston
I still have no idea how the folks in the band who were in relationships pulled it off. I tried dating. It didn't work out too well.

Panos "Feast" Hodges
I remember hearing how the album sounded mastered, and being really excited about it.

Diane Ost

The one downside to the process of getting the record done was the cover art falling through. Eventually, we just asked Panos, which we should have done from the outset. He'd done the art for the seven inch, and he ended up doing art for everything we did after that, even after he left the band.

Panos "Feast" Hodges

I drew this guy in a suit and tie throwing his briefcase off of a bridge and shouting, "THE ALPHANUMERIC MURDERS!" Kind of a Derek Hess meets Raymond Pettibon thing. It was weird, but it worked.

Thirteen: A Quintet, Again

The memory of their brief time as a quintet had stayed in the backs of several members' minds. When the opportunity arose to again become a five-piece, they seized it.

Curt Allston
Dean had a friend named Virgil Carey. Nice guy, really quiet. You know how you'd see the word "affable" in old books and you'd think that you'd never have cause to use it? Well, that guy gave me a reason, because Virgil Carey was really fucking affable. He and Dean had been friends for a while–you know that–and he ended up introducing Dean to Marco Hodge. I think their families were friends or something.

Diane Ost
We were starting to change up our sound a little bit. Dean and I wanted more straight-up noise in the band. Instead of the clean guitar/distorted guitar thing we'd had before, we thought that we could have one that was just a wall of sound. He called it "the rocketship effect."

Panos "Feast" Hodges
I remember Dean was listening to a lot of dub around then. I blame Fugazi.

Marco Hodge (guitar, 1996-1999)
My dad had been friends with Virgil Carey's mom since before either of us were born. He was this angry liberal priest–marched everywhere there was to march in the 60s, homesteaded for a while. I work in tech now. I think he might hate me.

Diane Ost
Dean suggested we jam with Marco one day, and this time out, it clicked.

Marco Hodge
My mom loved free jazz. I grew up listening to John Coltrane's *Interstellar Space*. That was what I thought music was, so the first time I heard Casey Kasem and *American Top 40*, I was terrified. Whenever I was in school with people, I had to remember that most people I met didn't know anything about the kind of music I was listening to. Even the punk kids in high school didn't know Derek Bailey, you know?

Diane Ost
The first time we did an interview with a zine after Marco joined, he kept talking about the records he was listening to. When we saw the interview in print, there was an absurd amount of typos.

Panos "Feast" Hodges
I remember him being a little weird, but fun. And maybe a year or two older than the rest of us, back when that counted for something.

Marco Hodge
I practiced with the band a few times, and it seemed to work out. I liked everyone. Virgil vouched for the members of the band. I had a solo noise project that I did in my basement, so it was nice for me to have something more structured happening as well. At that age, I really liked the idea of coming in and fucking with someone's verse-chorus-verse. In my mind, that was what I was doing. Even though, soon enough, I was writing some stuff with them that had verses and choruses and verses.

Panos "Feast" Hodges
I remember he clicked pretty well with all of us. Especially Curt. They seemed to get it on a pretty innate level.

Marina Ito
Apparently they had a song written as a five-piece within three weeks of Marco joining the band.

Julia Wittimer
I got to see one of the first shows with Marco in the band. It was weird seeing what the band had evolved into–they were a stranger thing

than when I'd been in it, but it was also gratifying to see that it wasn't just...someone playing the same parts that I'd played who wasn't me.

Diane Ost

Our summer tour started coming together. We figured we'd book some studio time once we got back, and redo an older song and record a few new ones. Someone always had a compilation they were putting together, it seemed like.

Fourteen: Shows and Sweat

Slowly, the band's touring ramped up, with their ambitions growing wider than the regional shows they'd been playing to date.

Panos "Feast" Hodges
I remember the record came out in April. It was snowing. Lightly, but still. We played a VFW hall in New Dutchess for about the three weeks that they did shows. It was a massive space, the PA that came with it sounded really good—and then some asshole broke a toiler paper dispenser and everything just fell apart. But our show was really fun, even if we sweated our asses off.

Curt Allston
What show of ours didn't we sweat at?

Diane Ost
We were, collectively, a very sweaty band.

Marco Hodge
I had never sweated much until I joined the band. I thought half of the band was going to die the first time we played. I thought that during most shows, too.

Marina Ito
The record release show for the self-titled record was one of the best shows they ever played. Top three, for sure. Outside of Virgil, I think I saw them more than anyone.

Diane Ost
The first show on that tour was on June first. We played in Delaware, at this really short-lived space. We did Delaware to Jersey to Hartford to Providence to New York City, so—it wasn't the most ass-backwards route we ever took.

Marco Hodge
We played [downtown New York City venue] Wetlands, which was fun.

Panos "Feast" Hodges
I remember the drive there. It was right next to the Holland Tunnel. You'd go inside and there was a van in one corner of it, covered with stuff. Half the calendar was punk shows and half was hippie stuff. I'd make the drive into see [Richmond, VA band] Avail like clockwork; they played there pretty regularly in those days.

Curt Allston
It was such a weird space, and it was always a challenge to get there and not end up going back through the Holland Tunnel to Jersey City.

Diane Ost
God, what if there was just a decoy version of Wetlands on the Jersey side of the Holland Tunnel?

Curt Allston
There were some cool spaces down there to see shows back then. I remember talking Polis into seeing Aphex Twin with me once. The guy was already an enthusiast, though I'm not sure why. Listened obsessively to Autechre.

Panos "Feast" Hodges
I remember Dean having some of the most random listening habits I'd ever seen circa the mid-90s. I have no idea what prompted it. Some of the stuff he was listening to, we were all listening to. And some of it...

Diane Ost
I'm pretty sure Virgil pointed him in the direction of some of the more electronic stuff he was listening to back then. Most of us listened to a lot of punk and very little else. We ended up going to some weird places, but samplers and programmed beats didn't really factor into things.

Curt Allston

Now that I'm thinking about it, it's hard to stop thinking about that Aphex Twin show. We were walking on all these pedestrian bridges over crosswalks around the tunnel. Polis was freaking out. He kept talking about "musical geography" like he was stoned. He wasn't stoned, or if he was, he wasn't sharing. We got to the show, and it was such a different crowd than what we were used to. I'm pretty sure we were the only two people there who'd ever been in a circle pit. Maybe not. These things surprise you.

Fifteen: Summer Tour, 1996

In the summer of 1996, the Alphanumeric Murders spent several weeks on the road in support of the album. It was a time during which certain band dynamics solidified, and the future pursuits of some of its members came into focus.

Diane Ost
That tour in the summer of 1996 was the only foolproof tour we had. The van didn't explode. No one had much personal drama. No one melted down. The label got the word out pretty well, too—we'd see posters around with the cover art in canary yellow. It looked like Pushead doing Beat Happening cover artwork or something.

Panos "Feast" Hodges
I remember being really bummed that we didn't have better tour stories. I'd read *Get in the Van*. I wanted good tour stories!

Marco Hodge
If I was to put a time to it, my guess is that that was when Dean started to think about composing music—or at least, something that was different than what we were doing. *Really* different. I'd see him in the back of the van with this tiny keyboard, with headphones on, just in his own world.

Diane Ost
That might've seemed aloof with someone else, but for us, it was just Dean being Dean. You know.

Panos "Feast" Hodges
I remember Dean raising every used LP bin he could find for, like, old Glenn Branca and Rhys Chatham recordings.

Marco Hodge
He was educating himself.

Diane Ost
We were on the road for thirty-four days. There were five of us, plus the occasional roadie. We all had very different approaches to hygiene. But that was par for the course for a touring band.

Panos "Feast" Hodges
I remember, after the tour, Dean would have these tapes, with short things on them that he'd made. Melodies and sketches. Every once in a while he'd talk to some of us about recording parts of them. He didn't play favorites or anything–he asked pretty much everyone who was in the band at various points. It wasn't that these would be new Alphanumerics songs. They were a side project. It was the start of something.

Curt Allston
It's funny. No one else from the band has done much with music since the band broke up. Julia did, but we never really hung out. But people know Dean, even if it's mostly a bunch of under-45 *New Yorker* readers. But because of that, I keep thinking of that tour in terms of how it affected Dean, and less about how it affected me. And I met my wife on that tour! We played in Austin with her band and we really hit it off and stayed in touch and ended up both in Portland in 2002. And we were married a year later! But my memories of that tour aren't about what I did. They're about him. I'm in the background of my own story. Are you finding that, too?

Sixteen: After the Tour, an EP

And then the tour was over. When the band returned home, the studio again called out to them, and another important working relationship for the band took hold.

Diane Ost
That always feels like the definitive Alphanumerics lineup for me. The 1996 tour, in terms of people, mostly, and chemistry. Even someone like Marco, who hadn't been there from the beginning–his enthusiasm played a big part in the sound. I mean, later, when Brandon joined, it felt like everyone's little brother was in the band. We all knew him when he was this thirteen-year-old kid at shows. It didn't help that Panos was a hard presence to replace in the band. In retrospect, I sort of wonder if we shouldn't have called it a day when he left. I'm getting ahead of myself, though.

Curt Allston
When we got back from the tour, we decided to record a seven inch. We wanted a different studio experience, and...you know where this is going, but I'll say it for the record. We had a lead on this guy, who you know, Will Morgan, who'd played in a bunch of weird avant-rock bands in the 70s and had a studio set up in his basement. We figured it would be worth giving him a shot. And he was local, which didn't hurt.

Panos "Feast" Hodges
I remember thinking that the fact that he wasn't a hardcore guy was appealing. We listened to a couple of records he'd played on, and they were certainly noisy and abrasive and everything else, but he'd recorded a whole lot more.

Curt Allston
Plans were afoot for album number two. We figured this would be a

good dry run for that–see if maybe this time we could have a better studio experience, and then use that as the starting point for something.

Marco Hodge
I was stoked, basically. The guy was one of my musical heroes back then. He still is.

Marina Ito
It's funny. Is this weird? Sorry if it's weird. I'd interviewed Will Morgan a few years earlier for a class project. He was kind of a weird local celebrity–some of the smarter alt-rock and college rock bands cited his old band as an influence, so there'd be a blip on the radar here and there. I mean, there wasn't much else happening around New Dutchess back then.

Marco Hodge
We really wanted him to do something on the EP. We had three songs ready to go, and we figured the fourth could be something we wrote in the studio. We kept asking Dean to play keyboards; we figured maybe one of the things he was writing in the back of the van could be turned into something for the record. Little did we know.

Diane Ost
We sounded really good on those recordings. Never quite got Mr. Morgan in there, though. A polite demurral.

Panos "Feast" Hodges
I remember stepping out of the studio. It was late August, and we'd watch the sky turning weird shades of blue as the sun set. It felt good to be in that space with everyone.

Curt Allston
I love how that record sounds. We ended up calling it *Low Energy*. It was Dean's idea. Hovercraft released it on seven inch and CD. They added some live tracks to the latter to fill it up.

Panos "Feast" Hodges
I remember the fall was pretty quiet.

Diane Ost
We did a couple of weekend trips. Boston, Philly, DC. We played New York again when the EP came out. We kept talking about Buffalo or Syracuse or even New Paltz, but it never totally happened. Dean and Marina moved in together somewhere in there.

Curt Allston
And then we were in 1997, and everything fell apart.

Seventeen: Prelude to a Collapse

In 1997, after their most productive year as a band, the members of the Alphanumeric Murders unexpectedly began drifting apart. The schisms that would open would alter the band in a series of dramatic ways.

Marina Ito
So it went like this. As of January 1997, I was in college and Dean was in college. We were living in Lambertville and commuting to Trenton State. Dean would talk about grad school sometimes, but he was never too clear about where. He had options, I'll say that. Marco was in the middle of some intense music studies program outside of New Brunswick. Diane was commuting to Stevens in Hoboken and working part-time at a studio near Clifton. And Panos was acting like a productive member of society. Curt was at William Paterson. So the band was there, and they were flexible. But it seemed like there were factions all of a sudden. Contingents.

Marco Hodge
Things got weird. We weren't all practicing together anymore. It was bits of us, playing in twos and threes. We had a small practice space, not far from the middle of New Dutchess. It was in this big warehouse that someone built when they thought the train would run through town. We called the space Belief, because we were assholes.

Panos "Feast" Hodges
I remember, for some reason, my schedule and Curt's lined up the best, so we'd hang out a lot. Practice together, get these really intricate things worked out. We savaged our speakers. It made a lot of sense to us, anyway.

Marina Ito
Marco more or less ended up moving in with us. We had a lot of dinners together. This is weird to say, but I think Dean worked best

when he had a sidekick around. His friend Virgil had just transferred out of state for the last couple of years of his degree, and I think Dean missed that rhythm. Maybe I'm wrong.

Diane Ost
The rehearsals that were just me, Dean, and Marco got weird. The energy was weird: we could kind of approximate the band in a very skeletal way. I was listening to a lot of bands like that–Hoover records and Rodan records and June of 44–where it wasn't about melody, it was about sinew and this sense of something ominous. Which, in retrospect...

Curt Allston
We kept joking that the band was going to turn into two side projects.

Panos "Feast" Hodges
I remember the full band would get together most every week, or every ten days. We laid low that winter. We rehearsed a lot and wrote a lot. We figured we'd get ready for the next album.

Diane Ost
We were already talking about titles. *Miners* was one of them. I don't know why.

Marina Ito
At dinner one night, Marco started talking shit about Curt, and I noticed that Dean didn't really defend him. That probably should have told me that things were getting weird within the band. But, I mean, it wasn't my band. I had my own things I was working on.

Diane Ost
It was late February, and we had our first show scheduled in a while. We were getting ready for a show in a few weeks at a VFW hall in Bound Brook. The really sad thing in retrospect was, we sounded great that practice. The old songs sounded fresh and the new songs were coming together. Couldn't ask for anything more than that.

Curt Allston
Somewhere in there, Marco asked me about a particular chord. Or he suggested I wasn't playing it well enough. I don't know.

Marco Hodge
I told Curt his playing was sloppy. The whole point of us both being in the band was for what we were doing to compliment one another. And it wasn't. The two of us sounded like something falling apart, and not in a good way.

Panos "Feast" Hodges
I remember everything basically stopped, and tempers flared up.

Diane Ost
It started out like any argument within the band. We'd had plenty, by that point.

Panos "Feast" Hodges
I remember nobody stepped in to try to calm people down, and that was a mistake. Things kept escalating.

Marco Hodge
It's been well over ten years, and I still don't think I was wrong, I shouldn't have let it go where it went.

Curt Allston
That fucking prick shouted at me for ten minutes, and I just gave up. I threw down my guitar, like—"What do you want me to do?"

Diane Ost
Marco called Curt's bluff, basically. And then Curt took a swing at him. Marco swung back. Panos grabbed Curt and Dean grabbed Marco, and I figured that was that. Dean and I tried to calm things down.

Panos "Feast" Hodges
I remember thinking at that point that things could still be salvaged.

Diane Ost
And then Marco told Panos he thought he was a shitty bass player.

Panos "Feast" Hodges
I remember looking around the room and thinking, you know what? Fuck it. I've done this long enough. If no one's going to calm him down, I'm out. I didn't walk out immediately, but, yeah, that was it for me.

Diane Ost
The rest of us asked Curt to leave the next day.

Curt Allston
Do I miss it? No. There were other bands out there.

Marco Hodge
As it was all happening, I remember this voice in my head saying, "This is the last band you're ever going to play in." And I was okay with that.

Diane Ost
We told Marco that he was on probation, and then Dean and I holed up and tried to figure out what the fuck we were going to do. We thought maybe that was it for the band. We were already making plans for the tour and for the next album, and I don't think either of us was ready for the band to be over at that point. So we kept on with it.

Eighteen: New Blood

In the second half of the year, the Alphanumeric Murders added a number of new faces.

Marco Hodge
It was a strange time. We didn't have a lot of leads on bassists and guitarists. And at that point, Dean was pretty adamant about us remaining a five-piece.

Diane Ost
Marco was a big proponent of stripping things back down. Dean liked the idea of balance. I think he used the phrase "sonic symmetry" once, and I almost slapped him. But I could see his point, and I don't think the songs we were working on would have worked with only one guitar. As for me, I just wanted to start playing again.

Marina Ito
I knew a couple of people. There was this post-hardcore band from Cherry Hill called Outfitter who'd just broken up, and their bassist was a friend of a friend. Nelson Cort was his name. I knew he was looking to play, and he kept talking about wanting to move north, so it seemed like a decent fit.

Nelson Cort (bass, 1997-1998)
I'd seen the band play a couple of times over the years and was really just excited to join.

Marco Hodge
We jammed with Nelson a couple of times. He figured out the bass parts pretty well, so that was good.

Diane Ost

We cancelled the Bound Brook show after the implosion, but we had a few more booked that we were hoping to play. In theory, we could have done them as a four-piece–Dean and I had a worst-case scenario mapped out, but we didn't want it to come down to that.

Marco Hodge

At some point, I remembered that my second cousin had been in a band once, and I reached out to her.

Diane Ost

Mina Sharpe. Ah, Mina. I assume she said about two words to you about her time in the band? That sounds about right.

Marco Hodge

Wilhelmina Sharpe has my favorite name of any human being I've ever met. She was maybe a year out of high school at the time. She'd grown up in Delaware and had moved to Jersey to study at Rider University.

Nelson Cort

I would get flustered around her because I had a crush on her. I don't know if anyone else in the band knew.

Marco Hodge

Nelson's crush was terrible.

Wilhelmina Sharpe (guitar, 1997-1999)

The music was fun, and playing in the band was fun, except for Nelson being totally awkward around me all the damn time. And that's about all I have to say about that.

Diane Ost

Look, for all that Mina and I disagreed, and we did, she was a fine musician, and the five of us gelled very well.

Marina Ito
I'd hear from Dean about how things were going. No new songs yet, he'd tell me. That was his benchmark: were they writing anything new? That seemed weird to me. There were already plenty of new songs happening before things got shaken up.

Diane Ost
The first show with the new lineup was at the Manville Elks Lodge. We were third of four. Normally, we'd have been fine with that, but we were nervous about how things would gel. We were apprehensive about expectations.

Marco Hodge
Dean felt the need to get a little crazy onstage, I think. Especially for that show. I don't know if that was because he was tense from not having played in so long. Maybe he was being cynical, and figured that if Mina and Nelson weren't quite there yet, no one would notice.

Marina Ito
I think it went really well. Dean had more presence than he usually did. He kept jumping off the stage and back on. Turns out that Mina Sharpe was an utterly terrifying figure at shows. She would just glare at random people in the audience, like she was going to kick their heads in.

Diane Ost
It was a huge relief. We got a response, for one, and that the lineup worked in front of a crowd. We all knew of bands—really, we knew bands, period—where certain people would quit and new people would come in, and it wouldn't work. The energy would be different, or there just wouldn't be energy. For us, it felt like a revival.

Marco Hodge
A lot of things got solidified after that. We booked some more local shows—we got something at Wetlands, and the First Unitarian Church in Philadelphia. And we locked down time for more recording.

Marina Ito

In April, Dean proposed to me. That changed things a little bit–some of the other people in the band were in relationships, but nothing that serious.

Marco Hodge

I announced it at the next show.

Nelson Cort

I was really happy for them! It was nice.

Diane Ost

We thought we'd do five weeks on the road in the summer, but that fell through. Then we had this wildly ambitious plan to go to California and back in three weeks, with a lot of overnight drives. We played a fest in San Diego, and we didn't want to miss that. Remember Jolt Cola? We drank a lot of it.

Marco Hodge

Three weeks out and back and getting ready to record with Will Morgan. Then we did a short tour down to Gainesville and back. That carried us through to the fall. That was basically our 1997.

Nineteen: The Difficult Second Album

The making of the second Alphanumeric Murders album found them wholly reinventing their working process.

Diane Ost
Hovercraft sent us some money for the second album. Booking time proved a little more complicated than we'd hoped, though.

Marco Hodge
We'd hoped to do two weeks straight in Will Morgan's studio. Turns out that he had a bunch of short sessions booked out that summer, so we ended up doing five days at one point and then nine days about a month and a half later. We set aside a little more time for mixing, too. After working with him for the EP, we knew that would be important. You probably know that, too.

Marina Ito
I asked Dean one night if they had a title for this. He wanted to call it *Bygone Tracks*, after one of the newer songs. I told him I didn't like it, that it sounded boring. I think the exact phrase was, "That sounds like something with a banjo on it." And now I own four banjos and play in a bluegrass band on the weekends. There's irony for you.

Nelson Cort
One day we were hanging out after practice in New Dutchess and I saw the shell of the hotel that overlooked the river. I said to Dean, "What's with the river skeleton?" His eyes lit up.

Diane Ost
Album number two: *Skeleton River*. Done.

Nelson Cort
I guess that's my lasting contribution to music. I'll take it.

Marco Hodge
Dean was starting to fuck around with field recordings back then. Sometimes he'd go below a bridge and listen to the traffic go by. Sometimes he'd go to the city and walk through crowds and get bits of conversation so fragmented it sounded like a collage. Sometimes he'd go for the most banal thing possible–though that might be me interpreting things after the fact.

Diane Ost
We brought it all in with us.

Marco Hodge
We gave a lot of it to Will Morgan and said, "Go nuts." Dean had some notes on the stuff he liked, but mostly, we left him to it.

Will Morgan (recording engineer)
I liked the freedom of it. They weren't the first band to do something like that, but I appreciated them wanting to try new things.

Diane Ost
I mean, we were nominally a hardcore band. Hardcore wasn't always the most creative thing. The big Refused album [1998's *The Shape of Punk to Come*] was still a ways off, and...yeah.

Marco Hodge
None of us wanted an album that was just the live show but cleaner. We all liked weird records.

Diane Ost
I think both sessions went really well.

Will Morgan
Both of the sessions went well. They were a fun group to work with.

Marco Hodge
We had a good feeling about things.

Will Morgan

I snuck in some guitar there. I'd started playing again after a long time off, and—it was nice to throw a few pieces into the mix.

Diane Ost

It was just Dean and I for the mixing, really.

Nelson Cort

I was really happy when I heard that album, when it was all done. I was really proud to have been a part of the group that made it.

Marco Hodge

It can be hard to distance yourself from something like that when you've been a part of it. But it was incredibly exciting to hear those songs, in that form, for the first time. The field recordings especially—they sounded great. The rhythms that had been picked up in those sounds blending in with the rhythms we were making...

Diane Ost

We were very excited. It sounded like our favorite records, but it also didn't.

Marco Hodge

You can certainly hear elements of what Dean went on to do, and what I went on to do. And if you put parts of it alongside some of the experimental solo stuff he was working on, I'm pretty sure you could find similarities as well. I'm sort of surprised no one's done that yet—that stuff's not hard to find. But at the same time, it didn't feel like a hardcore band playing a composer's side project. We were a proper band, and we were a good one.

Twenty: Changes Continue

Early in 1998, the band's newfound stability was again put into jeopardy.

Diane Ost
So we were all really excited about things, and then Nelson quit the band a couple of weeks into 1998.

Nelson Cort
I just really wanted to be a youth pastor, you know? And I loved the sound of this band, but it wasn't really what I wanted to be doing.

Marco Hodge
I never understood that guy.

Diane Ost
Finding a replacement for Nelson wasn't too hard. We ended up finding this guy Brandon Gray, who was a really nice kid. He was nineteen and looked sixteen and that led to some hilarious moments—sorry, "hilarious," like in scare quotes—because one time the cops pulled us over because they thought we were kidnappers.

Brandon Gray (guitar, 1998-1999)
I can neither confirm nor deny that I ever played in anything called the Alphanumeric Murders. Wouldn't be good for the brand.

Marina Ito
There wasn't a huge shift in style when Brandon joined. He was, maybe, a little more melodic in his playing than Nelson, but not that much. And the band was really focusing on being tight when they played the songs; they weren't really writing anything new.

Diane Ost
We were getting very efficient in our practices, in those days. I was usually there first. Marco and Wilhelmina would show up together,

then Dean, then Brandon. Sometimes I'd get to the practice space and Dean would be there already, working on his own stuff.

Marco Hodge
It was interesting: Dean was being somewhat public about working on other things at that point. He'd talk about it in interviews. But he was also pretty adamant that this wasn't a side project, that he wasn't playing shows, anything like that.

Marina Ito
In those days, hardcore was still its own relative system. If you were in a hardcore band and did something else, people would pretty often consider that a hardcore band as well, no matter what it sounded like.

Marco Hodge
We played the Masonic Temple in Metuchen a couple of times, and there was a record store not too far from there. They broke everything down by genre: a rock section and a punk section and an industrial section and a folk section. But if you'd been in a punk band and made a country record, it would still be filed under punk. I think Dean was very aware of that.

Twenty-one: Life Changes, Band Stability

Higher education ended and married life began.

Diane Ost
A few of us were finished with college that May, so the plan was to head out on the road after that. Hovercraft set an April release date for the album. We set some shows up; we had a pretty good sense of how it worked by then.

Marina Ito
Somewhere in there Dean and I were set to get married. We were looking at a September wedding.

Marco Hodge
We played a lot of shows when I was in the band, that's for sure. The only regret I have is that we never made it to Europe. A couple of friend bands did. There was a little talk of that in the fall, that we'd maybe fly over and do a couple of weeks. But Polis paused for a while; I think that was the one time in his life where he prioritized something else over music. He said that he was trying to figure things out, that he'd be newly married, that he didn't want to split for that long right after his wedding. Totally understandable, as far as I'm concerned, but still.

Panos "Feast" Hodges
I remember every now and then Dean and I would meet up for dinner or coffee. It took a couple of months after I left the band for that routine to resume, but it did. Sometimes Virgil Carey would be along, too, if he was in town on a break or something. We would go to a diner and drink a ton of coffee and talk about the shit guys in their early twenties talk about. Virgil was already working part-time at a nonprofit in Lambertville; whenever we'd hang out with him he'd talk about all the cool shit you could do on the internet. Virgil knew more about

that than a lot of people. Virgil had his internet plans and Dean had his New York plans. Me? I had coffee.

Marina Ito
Dean and I were talking about moving to New York in the fall. I was looking into getting a job there; it seemed like he could still do the band pretty easily. We had some things figured out.

Diane Ost
Getting the second album figured out was easier than we thought. The first album had the illustration; the second one had a photo that Julia Wittimer had taken of the New Dutchess skyline, such as it was. We kept it in the family.

Marco Hodge
The band's name in white, the album's title in red next to it.

Julia Wittimer
It was nice to contribute to the band from another angle. It was also strange seeing them again. My band had played a few shows with them, but half the time that was us crossing paths on tour, or at a fest somewhere. And it was weird seeing a version of the band where I didn't know half the members. Felt kinda like going back to your old high school a few years after you graduate, you know?

Marco Hodge
Somewhere in there, we figured we'd set some dates with Will Morgan to record again, in late 1998. Maybe I'm getting ahead of myself.

Diane Ost
We toured that summer. It was weird; I don't think we realized that *Skeleton River* was clicking with people until we played spaces in Washington State and Arizona and Texas and a fuck of a lot of kids knew our songs. We headlined a lot.

Marina Ito
I roadied for the band that summer. The van had a weird balance: me

and Dean, Diane doing the bulk of the driving, Brandon just writing in his notebooks and saying three words a day, and Marco and Mina being antisocial. There were factions. Not in a bad way.

Diane Ost
It was a very weird tour. We didn't fight a lot, which was rare. Still, there were groups. I would drive or I'd sit shotgun and read or I'd be driving.

Marco Hodge
We knew a lot of bands who had problems touring: their albums wouldn't be ready, or their merch wouldn't be ready, or their van would completely break down. We avoided all of that.

Diane Ost
I almost wish we'd had some trouble.

Marco Hodge
I think maybe it would've built character. This whole thing would be more fun. "And then we broke down in Montana and the wolves attacked, and we had to set our guitars on fire to fight them off." That's fun! That's entertaining. We did not do that.

Diane Ost
The thing is, we were lucky. We all got along on tour, our records got to the right people, our van never had too many problems. Do I wish I had more stories about being lost on the Upper Peninsula? Sure. But in the end, I was in a band that people tell me mattered to them, and matters to them. That's a good thing.

Twenty-two: The Fall

Dean Polis and Marina Ito were married on September 26, 1998.

Marco Hodge

It was a fine wedding. It ended up being in an outdoor space near the river. Dean's mother rented out a hall for the reception. Good music was played.

Diane Ost

Lots of dancing. Lots of silliness. I'm pretty sure Dean's friend Vigil got drunk and tried to flirt with me. That was a little sad, but endearing.

Marina Ito

We honeymooned in Iceland. Why not?

Diane Ost

So this was how things stood in the fall. Dean and Marina were looking at places in the city. Marco was trying to figure out his next step as far as academics were concerned. We were writing songs, but they were different—Dean was starting to contribute more of the melodies, not just the lyrics. The songs, at this point, were written by Marco and Dean and I. Nelson and Wilhelmina didn't really contribute much.

Marco Hodge

The new songs we were writing were very different. There was a lot more dissonance, and more time shifts. We tried a few out, and we got a lot of stares.

Diane Ost

Something seemed to be shifting, but I still can't tell exactly what that was. We were all happy with the songs. They were fun to play. We were all looking forward to recording with Will Morgan again.

Marina Ito

They had a title going in, which was a first for them. The plan was to call it *Untitled New Dutchess Album*, which in retrospect seems incredibly pretentious, but seemed amazingly witty at the time.

Marco Hodge

We knew going into it that the album would be short. We figured eight songs; we had eleven total written. We figured we'd have an album, a seven inch, and maybe a compilation track. As it turns out, we were right.

Diane Ost

We were recording the album over a week in late November, which is my favorite time of the year. It was the first time we recorded in that studio when it wasn't sweltering. I remember a lot of standing in the back yard, drinking cider, and watching the sky turn darker shades of blue. The platonic ideal of Jersey autumn, basically.

Marco Hodge

As we were putting the album together, we started to feel like this might be our last album, and that started to feel more and more like an open secret as we recorded things. There was a sense of finality, a sense of making things count.

Diane Ost

It felt like we had taken this band as far as it could go. If we did anything else, it wouldn't be this band, essentially.

Marco Hodge

I think we all just knew.

Marina Ito

Dean would come home from recording and look both satisfied and sad.

Diane Ost

The funny thing was realizing that we were in a band that had more former members than current members. That isn't a rule of thumb for calling it a day, but maybe it should be.

Marco Hodge
At a practice a couple of weeks after mixing the album, we finally formally said that we were breaking up. There wasn't any argument.

Twenty-three: The End and
the Aftermath

Plans began for the band's final shows.

Diane Ost
We talked with Hovercraft early in the new year and told them we
were calling a day. We figured we'd have our last show in March. Why
make people sweat more than they had to?

Marco Hodge
No one really knew what would happen with *Untitled New Dutchess
Album*. We didn't know if they'd do it or tell us to go somewhere else.
We had an audience, but it wasn't that big of one.

Diane Ost
In the end, it came out in the fall. We were pleasantly surprised.

Marina Ito
The Alphanumeric Murders played their last show at the Court Tavern
in New Brunswick on March 21, 1999. It was a Sunday matinee, which
seemed appropriate. There were two openers. The Alphanumerica
played for an hour and a half, and played what seemed like every song
they'd ever written.

Diane Ost
It was a weird way to split up, but we were parting ways as friends.
That was important. We could all still hang out; we all might make
more music together, we thought.

Marco Hodge
The new songs still baffled people. I think we played five of the songs
from the last session in the last show, and the room was quieter. When

that album did come out, suddenly a lot of people "got it" who hadn't remotely beforehand. I think one review called us "tremendously underappreciated," which was bullshit.

Diane Ost
The weirdest part about the last show, I think, was playing each song and then thinking, "Well, that's it." That sense that you've played that piece of music for the last time. Half of me was endorphins and half was just this bittersweet feeling that lasted for days afterwards.

Marina Ito
People flew in from Oregon and Colorado for that show.

Panos "Feast" Hodges
I remember it was fun being there for the last show. But it was also really strange to be watching them be played. Muscle memories still endured.

Julia Wittimer
I never stopped playing music. Weirdly, Diane and I ended up in the same band for about two months six years after the last Alphanumerics show. That was fun. I wish it had lasted longer.

Marco Hodge
Somewhere along the way, I stopped playing the guitar. There's other music, and other music I make. But guitars? It's like an allergy.

Curt Allston
I ended up working in the music industry for a while. Classic punk turned capitalist. Now, I work in tech. Doesn't everyone?

Diane Ost
I play in bands and I teach. It keeps me busy.

Emmet Foster
I work as a biochemist in Texas. I like that life.

Panos "Feast" Hodges

I'm an ex-straight-edge kid who runs a small craft brewery. No one saw that coming, but also everyone saw that coming.

Marina Ito

Dean and I moved to New York a little later than expected, but we got there. I moved to Hudson a few years ago. I like it there. It's quiet.

Diane Ost

Every once in a while, one of us will joke about a reunion show. We've gotten a few offers. We talked about it once when were getting drinks after our friend Virgil's memorial. But I don't think anything's going to come of it. And if it did, I don't know who would actually be in that version of the band. But hey, anything's possible.

FIVE

NEARSIGHTED IN NORTHERN CITIES

(1994)

WINTERLIGHT ON WILL MORGAN. It always disoriented him, the fact that the day had endured despite time spent inside a cavernous space, that the afternoon's last gasp was still bright enough to sting. A walk through glass doors and onto the sidewalk; four p.m. on a Saturday in February, 1993. He was in the middle of his annual Hartford trip, the eighth he had made in as many years. Some years it felt like routine, the way he used to feel moving from chord to chord, the ecstatic familiar. Other times it's tradition, greetings and updates recited by rote. First hockey, always with Falk and Patten, before they got into their car and ventured back to their apartment just north of the city. Then Will would make his way down the block for a short coffee with Barrett; and then, the drive back south, towards western New Jersey. For the first few years they had occupied a quartet of seats, never too close to the ice. And then one year, Barrett had been absent, and neither Falk nor Patten had seen fit to address the matter.

Now the farewells outside of the arena. The perennial invitation to Falk and Patten that, should they ever be in or around western Jersey, they should visit. Will knew that it was implausible: Falk's professorial duties and Patten's field research occupied their time to an almost comedic extent. And yet the offer must be made, and must be made annually. A frost-laced wind coasted across Will's face as he watched his friends walk down the sidewalk. He breathed warm air into his fists and rubbed his palms over exposed ears and mapped the way to Barrett's chosen coffee spot.

Will made a careful adjustment of his glasses. Åsa's of an age to watch over herself now, he told himself. Well-behaved, not likely to run riot over the place or open the doors to some afternoon's revelry.

How different she is than the punks he knew, thought Will.

Will Morgan at the bar in Hartford, a four p.m. beer before him. Beside him was Barrett, cheeks emblazoned with a younger man's sideburns. What's left of the day still streamed through the windows, but it was dwindling, the month still choking sun's access to streets.

"I don't see Åsa's mother much anymore," he was saying, and wondered why Barrett has led him down this path. Wondered what Barrett is doing in a bar to begin with: he'd been sober the last time they'd met, and Will had felt a shock when Barrett met him outside the coffee shop and jabbed a neutered thumb to the neon signs across the street. "Let's go there," Barrett had said, and Will nodded. "I'm only down for one," Will had said. "Long drive ahead of me, and a longer night when I get where I'm going."

Later, their drinks down to a quarter full, he reiterated it. "I've got somewhere I need to be," said Will.

"I don't," said Barrett.

A look at his watch outside of the bar. 6:05. Menachem Jennings had told him to be at Coney Island High on St. Marks Place for the show by 8:30; time enough for a coffee before the drive.

A quarter for the payphone. Thirty seconds on the line with Åsa, making sure everything's fine. The sky had gone past violet, and Will remembered his jacket in the car's back seat, the temperature slowly pushing towards freezing. Another farewell to Hartford, then. And in another year he would come back, will again gather with friends, will once more watch the Whalers play and then find Barrett and trade stories of the year just passed.

2

WILL HAD NEVER PLAYED MUSIC WITH MENACHEM, though the subject often came up when they spoke. Usually it came down to Will suggesting buses to his cohort, or offering to meet at a train station halfway between the city and New Duchess. Menachem came from a background of dissonance, of time spent abusing reeds even as he kept the brass curves of his saxophone meticulously aligned. Will would have been curious to improvise with him: to sit in the studio and let tape roll and see what emerged. "There's a guest room next to the live room," he always told Menachem. "I'm told it's all kinds of comfortable."

They had known one another for sixteen years now; had met at an art space in Tacoma where Will's old band had stopped on their final tour. Menachem had been one of the six members of the other group on the bill: a low-slung group called Jack-the-Sharp. They had taken some cues from The Stooges but preferred simply to drop their songs into a lower register and let them howl; Menachem's baritone sax, to Will the standout instrument, roared through most of their numbers, evoking images of the building's walls trembling towards implosion, footholds gone unsteady.

The two bands had played to a room of a dozen, three of those barely there, the rest attentive and appreciative. This was not a crowd on which social histories would have been made, and yet whenever Will read outsider accounts of Northwestern music or biographies off the beaten path, he always attuned himself for mentions of the space, of Jack-the-Sharp, of the night a quartet from Philadelphia by way of Iowa had passed through town. He always kept some eye on history, or at least his own hopes of it.

Menachem, for his part, had kept a recording of the night; had filed it away in a small room in Blissville that he visited every three weeks to check for dust and defects, to maintain some grand sort of integrity. One day, it might see formal release.

A few years ago, they had encountered one another by chance. Will had been enlisted as producer by a local four-piece, a contrast to his usual recording engineer gigs. He'd driven to Hoboken to watch them play at Maxwell's, had seen a familiar face in the crowd. Menachem was there in some loose capacity, managing one of the other bands on the bill or collaborating with someone who happened to be in the room. (Will's memory was hazy on that particular detail.) Will recognized him almost instantly: Menachem's temples now boasted a dusting of white, but other than that he looked much the same. Will, too, was recognizable from his road days: his hair still largely dark brown, his face cleanshaven. The primary difference in his appearance was the style of glasses he wore; for that show, he had adopted a wire-rimmed pair, more surgical than academic. They reminisced quietly in between guitar squalls and pinpoint rhythms.

Since then, they had remained in regular contact. Menachem's name had weight in certain circles, and he tended to route certain bands in his orbit towards Will's studio. For the past few years, this had been what had beckoned Will into the city: a recommendation from Menachem, whose instincts about Will's own taste in music was normally spot-on; trips to hear bands in the live setting before bringing them into the studio; trips to the Continental and Brownies and the Knitting Factory and Threadwaxing Space. And occasional stops in Hoboken, something of a halfway point for the two men to convene, Will adding miles on his '87 Jetta and dreading the sight of dented doors or shattered glass on the windowside sidewalk.

This evening, Menachem's advice pointed him to a club on St. Mark's Place. "It's quality punk rock," Menachem had told Will two days before. "Focused stuff. The singer's got a howl like you wouldn't believe, and there's something almost ambient about the guitarwork." The band—called Dead Spies—had cut a handful of demos, and were looking to release their first EP; a moderately-sized label in Massachusetts had signed them to a two-record deal, and they were eager to find an engineer. Hence: Will walking into the smaller performance space at Coney Island High and looking for Menachem at the bar. All he had to do, he noted, was look for the other person in the room over the age of forty.

He thought about Åsa, back in New Jersey. Inevitably, he thought of the strange tower that loomed over their town. It was easier now to do these trips than in years past. Those decisions: hire a sitter until late in the night or make the trip back to New Duchess early, skip out after three or four songs and hope he could form a sense of the band's right and proper sound from that fractional impression. The annual Hartford trip always struck him as the most potentially ruinous; memories came to Will now of the same drive seven years earlier, when traffic had morassed him on four separate pockets on the trip back home. Long still stretches punctuated by hasty trips into rest areas, feeding quarters into a pay phone and buying coffee to obtain more quarters. In recent years it had grown easier: Åsa now capable of looking after herself. There were still periodic check-ins from the road, usually a call on his way to Hartford and a call on the way back home. And yet now the trip to Hartford itself had grown awkward, the group he'd gone to meet now fragmented. Conversations at bars and at their seats watching the game, Will never sure whose names might bring stares and declarations of offhand contempt. Maybe that had been the swap: his daughter's self-sufficiency bartered for the dissolution of his bandmates' detente.

At the club, he found the back of the room and stood against it. Dead Spies would be the second of three bands; there was no sign of Menachem, and no indication of whether the first band had yet to play or had just finished their set. Amplifiers and a drum kit sat on the stage anonymously, a backline or the gear of a band not interested in identifying characteristics. The room was about a third full. Will gauged the average age at twenty-four or twenty-five; a different generation from his own, then. He had made albums older than most of the attendees here; he had worked with some of the bands he saw emblazoned on t-shirts and patches sewn onto backpacks.

He took off his glasses for a moment, wiped them on the corner of his shirt, then donned them again. In the gap before the next set, Television's second album piped through the speakers on stage. Will nodded his head in time with the rhythms.

He took off his glasses and watched the room become indistinct, gray shapes and blurred circles of color around the stage lights. It seemed more clear to him, in some ways, than his sight with glasses on. Though this might simply be intentional delusion, a way of thinking that made less and less sense the further it was considered. Will had had plenty of those over the course of his life. Sometimes he saw clouds as he surveyed what was before him. He suspected that cataracts were a decade off; his father and his uncles had all gone through procedures for their removal, and he saw his turn coming before long. Standing there in isolation on the club's back wall, a tripwire shudder passed through his thigh and up his back. He thought, *Plan for that now*. He saw a cost looming much as the cost of Åsa's future schooling might loom. He crossed from the wall to the corner of the bar, where a pitcher of water sat, took a small plastic cup from a stack beside the pitcher, and filled it. Waiting for Menachem, he removed his glasses, rubbed his eyes again, sought out details to carry with him from the room.

On the stage, musicians were gathering, emerging through the crowd on the floor to heft guitar cases and drum heads. Will stared at them; they looked familiar enough for him to conclude that this was, in fact, Dead Spies, and that he had missed the first band. Good, he thought; time enough to watch the band, to catch up with Menachem, and to be home before midnight. To, perhaps, talk briefly with Åsa–late at night, the clock chasing midnight, neither feeling much compulsion to sleep. Åsa had adopted his own sleeping habits, and he saw no need to scratch at the issue; the pursuit of late nights was not something he would opt to control.

These kitchen-table check-ins had become a strange tradition in the previous year and a half, so much so that Will was unsure how they'd gone without them. Åsa would be waiting, often writing, often in her own soundscapes, sometimes friends' bands' basement demos and sometimes music more official in its production. She would ask him about the groups he'd seen that night, and he would relay his account of the evening to her, sometimes jotting down notes as new angles on the group's sound occurred to him, touchstones for the recording sessions to come. Sometimes Åsa would jot something down as well on a small note or scrap of paper; sometimes Will would bring home a compact disc or cassette, might be tempted to move the conversation into another room and cue up a song. They would sit and trade accounts, with Åsa occasionally relaying tales of a basement or hall show from earlier in the day. Most of the time he would say, "I never much cared for hardcore," but sometimes she would bring him news of something more esoteric: Seattle punks who'd come to John Coltrane through unorthodox means, a D.C. trio who echoed the surf-rock he'd fallen in love with as a boy and the postpunk he'd fallen hard for just as Åsa's mother had moved out of his life; a storming dissonant group from Olympia whose guitars rendered fields, suggested depths, or simply hovered and therefore become transcendent.

It was time, Will thought, to take the pulse of the room. Ten minutes until Dead Spies would play, he figured. He'd see Menachem soon enough. On the wall opposite the bar, a few small tables selling CDs and seven inches and t-shirts, manned by band members and friends of the band, and currently serving no buyers. Will would be curious to see what happened once Dead Spies had concluded their set: would he see a rush towards that table, or would interest remain flat? Before they began playing, he would look to see what they had to offer; he would purchase a beer and stride to the table and look things over.

The space was filling up now. Will recognized some faces: a hand-ful of musicians he'd worked with in the past few years whom he planned to greet once the set was done, a smaller handful of industry types, and one or two bodies that he'd simply come to recognize over years of coming to shows. The man with prematurely white hair; the red-haired woman with four piercings too many; the rain-thin guy who Will had assumed was chronically ill until someone had set him straight. "Just vegan," the drummer in a post-hardcore band had once said to Will. "A vegan who doesn't know shit about nutrition. You know Goldberg's Peanut Chews? Those are vegan. Doesn't mean they should be the foundation of your diet."

He saw dark work jackets and a smaller number of sweaters worn by skinny bys with close-cropped hair. Drive Like Jehu t-shirts and someone in a hooded sweatshirt with SAMIAM emblazoned on the back. Some months Will would drive to the nearest record store, would seek out music he hadn't had cause to encounter on his own. Most of his friends, his former bandmates and old tourmates and prior clients, would say that they'd grown sick of it. He thought about that question of looking forward; he wished he had brought a notebook with him, to jot down the names on shirts, to delve further in. He knew he'd hate most of it, would find much of it uninteresting or simply retreading ground he'd heard covered years, decades earlier. Still, the pursuit beckoned.

One of the guitarists was now tuning, brittle notes coming through onstage speakers. The bassist, too—lower notes, fuller. Will thought about the last time he had played an instrument. Sometimes he would take it out, would play in the studio on quiet days. Sometimes he thought about multitracking; he could play cursory drums, could play a passable guitar, could even emanate a strange singing croak that a couple of friends had told him was better than he believed. He was never a songwriter, though, and the thought of assembling a one-man band to channel someone else never struck him as all that satisfying. He enjoyed that comfort, the familiar calm that came over him when he played with those he knew, that he trusted. When you didn't even need to look over to know what transition was coming, when you could feel it before it happened. He needed to get Menachem to come west, or get some faction of the old band—the Barrett faction or the Falk-and-Patten one—to do the same. Some familiarity; some response to a feeling that he hadn't summoned in years.

The drummer's impromptu soundcheck; the sound of beats in isolation. Now came the second guitarist to tune, eking out his own brittle notes. He tuned faster than the other, Will noted. He walked to the bar, downed five dollars, and walked back towards his spot on the wall with a handful of beer. The merch table caught his eye, and he wandered over, suddenly conscious of his age, of how this might look. A disjointing; a recognition of this irregular pathway, that most of those around him had not spent the afternoon watching hockey in Hartford.

Dead Spies, he saw, had one seven inch on the table. "Dreams With Wrong Solutions" was the a-side; "Live Moon" was the song on the reverse. He handed over three dollars in exchange for a copy, and held it by his side as he stood and waited for the group's set to begin. He'd move to the center of the room soon enough; would find where the sound was optimal and chase it there. Voices came, checking microphones, checking onstage levels. The bassist and both guitarists all offered up their own shouts, their own croons; and, in the case of one, a slight scream, *check*! transformed into a source of terror. Will heard it and wondered where it would come again; he knew, just as sure as the gun on the mantle, that it would certainly make an appearance.

And then, through the onstage monitors, the voice of the soundman: "That okay?" A nod from the bassist, who Will took to be the primary vocalist. "Whenever you're ready, then." Muted, the sort of conversation most here would overlook. Glances passed among the four on stage. Will heard something that sounded like, "Dreams or Rake?" A pause, then, from the bassist: "Dreams." And so it began.

One song in, the crowd was already too dense for Will to have any hope of seeing Menachem. Three-quarters of the room now full, dense dark fabrics and pale arms fluctuating in uneven rhythms. The band's songs stretched forward, rhythms ascending and beginning to fray, and then long languorous chords from one amplifier or another filtered in, encircled the rhythm, and pulled them back. It wasn't so much a question of dynamics, Will observed, as it was one of tension and release; something harder for him to capture in the studio, but something that could be captured, could be channeled.

The bassist sang out with a clear voice; one guitarist chimed in with yelps and shouts, and the other muttered along in a low counterpoint. The crowd embraced it, sometimes surging forward to meet the stage and sometimes giving way to shoves and kicks and shouts directed inwards. Will stood towards the back of the throng but was still in the movement, still deep enough in it that he was jostled and sometimes shoved with the outside edge of a forearm or the back of his hand. He downed the rest of his beer as quickly as he could and let the plastic cup drop. Two songs in the crowd began leaping onto the stage and then, just as quickly, off into the crowd, arms flailing ecstatically for that five or six or seven feet before the crowd carrying them lost strength or will or patience and lowered them back into its embrace. And Will watched it all and smiled and waited for the next song to begin.

A third of the way through the second song, stagediving commenced. Subtly at first, a few thin men bounding from the stage onto the hands of their compatriots, making it a few feet into the audience, and then righting themselves, taking their feet, and waiting for their turn to leap again. Fifteen or twenty feet separated the furthest they'd reached from the spot where Will stood, and he waited, his attention still captured by the sounds of the group more than any of the motions undertaken by the people watching them.

The third song found one guitar delving into deep bent rhythms above which sonorous vocal harmonies rested, the song's structure breaking down midpoint into an evocation of fragility, then ratcheting back up over a simple accelerating beat. The harmonies broke down into countermelodies, the lyrics naming items, details, dates and places and names, the crowd's energy accumulating and manifesting itself in leaps, in surges forward, in joyous shouts. "That was a new one," the bassist said as the song reached its end. Will realized he was nodding, as though the other half of a private conversation.

By the fourth song, the motion in the crowd ahead of him had turned more rhythmic, had become almost organized. Will found himself having to push back when some staggered back into his vicinity; his attention drifted from the band to the crowd, and he thought it best to move back towards the wall after this particular song. And then a repeat stagediver took a leap into the crowd and ecstatically made his way across palms of hands and forearms, his own arms flailing wildly and a look of utter bliss on his face. He was passed towards the back of the room faster than any of his predecessors had been, arms in motion like a kung-fu diagram. And soon enough he was on the shores of Will's space; Will's arms went up to move him along and instead Will found two strange fingers moving towards his face, found them catching the inside of his glasses, and then watched his glasses inadvertently flung into the middle of the motion before the stage. As the younger man passed over him, Will stared into the

venue's center with newly blurred vision and realized that said glasses were lost, were fucked, were gone, and that this meant something
new for the night.

At the end of that song he moved to the back of the room and
waited there, waited out Dead Spies' set, his attention no longer on
the music so much as on the large blurred mass before him, like a
psychedelic rendering of a cartoon dust storm. Low light and flashing
lights and boundless energy. At the end of their set he did a cursory
squatting search of the middle of the room. He found one lens intact
and little else: some shards of plastic and two twisted pieces of wire.
Expected perhaps in this moment to hear Menachem's voice, unexpected and possessing a sudden and pointed concern. Will did not
hear Menachem's voice; he noted to himself that he'd need to call him
in the coming days, would need to speak with him about the band,
would need to confirm days and rates. Would probably not want to
mention this, a note of dissonance in the proceedings that would
benefit no one in particular.

The crowd seemed to be making their final exits after Dead Spies'
set. Will felt for the band that would follow them; could certainly
understand their situation. And yet he knew that he'd also be exiting.
He needed to find a pay phone; he needed to find Åsa.

3

THIS, FOR WILL ON THIS PARTICULAR NIGHT, was the city at ten
p.m.: a series of blurred shapes and eternally bursting lights, objects
thinned at their outlines passing down the street, pedestrians distin-
guished by height and skin and very little else. Everything seemed
to lack distinctions: shapes fed into shapes, forms collapsed into one
another. And yet the clarity of colors bled into his eyes, taking hold of
his sense of balance, his notions of proportion. The lag of his vision
contrasting with the sense that these colors were somehow more true,
that the glass previously sitting between his eyes and the world was
somehow lessening his perception, that this reduction of focus was
somehow a gateway to a superior perception.

And then, as he continued down the block towards Third Avenue,
costs came to mind. He had cursory health coverage through the
studio, incorporated years before as much for Åsa's security as for his
own. Glasses were a different expense, though; one incurred every
three or four years; an expense for a boom time rather than one for
a fallow year. Which, Will reminded himself, this was not—the year
to come looked to be one of his busiest. And yet: these things that
seemed most assured often crumbled; bands broke up, feuded with
management; acquired new managers and found themselves chan-
neling new whims, sonic and otherwise.

As pedestrians passed him by, Will attempted to recall where his
previous pair of glasses had ended up; he anticipated his conversation
with Åsa, of her concerns and questions and began to outline his next
few steps. Did it make more sense for her to come to the city, for him
to guide her back to his parked car and for her to drive it home? Or
should he board a bus bound for New Duchess and meet her and
return to the city the following day to pick up his car? Meters might
expire, he realized; his vehicle might be impounded, dragged off to
some unknown lot in the outer boroughs, newfound expenses born

from indecision. The fact that he recognized it did nothing to halt the panic that crept through his stomach; instead, it prompted him to pause and to retreat deeper into the sidewalk, the blurred masses before him in constant ecstatic motion.

It was crucial to Will that he have a plan before telephoning Åsa. Driving home in his own condition was not an option; rather, it was an invitation to collision, to oblivion on the unlit roads on the outskirts of New Duchess once the interstate had been left behind. Was there a neighbor, a friend, a casual acquaintance whose car he could borrow once an older iteration of his glasses had been located? Or should he enlist Åsa as his courier, hope that a last bus might still depart from somewhere in New Duchess?

He could call and put the question to her himself; but as this thought crossed his mind it set him trembling. He would call, he realized. He would call and ask her to make the trip in, would meet her at the Port Authority and rely on her from that point on. He could stifle those intervening hours with transit and coffee, find a book to hold close to his eyes and scan until he heard Åsa's voice again. One deli yielded change for the meter two blocks off, and another yielded money for the telephone. He leaned in, eyes not far from finger not far from the pay phone's familiar grid. He heard the rings in one ear and awaited the sound of connection, the promise of communication.

4

WILL HADN'T TAKEN THE SUBWAY IN FOUR YEARS, not since he'd decided it was his duty to bring Åsa in to the city for a day's worth of culture. He had parked in the Village and had ushered Åsa to the 6 at Astor. They had begun the day at MoMA and gone north from there, then boarded the 6 again to usher Åsa further north to the Whitney. The line had then brought them back to SoHo; they had walked through several galleries, one of which hosted a group show in which work by an old tourmate of Will's could be seen. Will and Åsa got back to the car at eight that night, headed for the Lincoln Tunnel, and stopped at a diner on Route 3 forty minutes later, watching the delirious neon shiver as they approached. They sat in their booth and spoke of what they had seen. Twenty feet away, a group of regulars clustered around the diner's bar, and Will vowed to be on the road again before any of that particular group departed.

Will thought it best to take himself to the Port Authority on foot; what he remembered of the underground system involved long walks in the pedestrian tunnels near the Terminal, and from the timing of things, it seemed more advantageous to make the uptown traversal on foot. His arrival time might coincide neatly with Åsa's; and it seemed to him that the Port Authority at this time of night would be ill-suited to his half-blindness.

The cold surrounded him, but so long as he had motion on his side, he had warmth. He clutched the Dead Spies record to his hip and jammed both hands into his pockets and set off. And so he came to Astor Place and turned north on Fourth Avenue, the buildings on either side of him a softened kaleidoscopic array of flattened lights and diffused scale. It was both familiar and treacherously altered, the city's grounded geography all but vanished to him now.

He hadn't walked through New York in a long time. He wanted to observe facades, to say with some certainty that things had changed, but all he could perceive were the existence of lights and the form of crowds. And slowly, a specific fear entered him as he crossed Sixth Avenue on 23rd Street: that he might pass someone who recognized him, that since his vision lent everyone anonymity, that he might ignore someone signaling frantically or attempting to reconnect. There would be no reunions here—at least not until Åsa arrived to enhance his eyes. Rather, this walk might lead to reunion's opposite, to a failure of recognition prompting schisms and faltering bonds. The city loomed around him, its form degrading, the precision of its grids and the narratives spelled out on awnings and neon signs rendered unavailable to him.

He walked up Seventh Avenue to the high 20s and passed the Fashion Institute of Technology. He suddenly felt very much his age, utilitarian in a space designed to reward the precise usage of accessories and praise an alien form of luxury. Long coats and dresses hung in gallery windows, lit from behind; their silhouettes looked to Will like something almost robotic, forms set adrift, headless sentries foreshadowing some new baroque age. He cut west, first to Eighth and then to Ninth, on 31st Street, letting the structures that squatted there loom over him like some modern leviathans. For a brief moment as he passed the western entrance to Penn Station, he wished that he had asked Åsa to take the train instead—had told her to call a cab to bring her the twenty miles to the closest station and use that as her point of departure. But the economics of that struck him suddenly and his second-guessing recoiled; he passed the white fleece of the post office at Eighth and crossed the next long block.

Little was open in the Port Authority by the time Will arrived: one coffee stand, at which he bought a brackish cup; a bar that looked unappealing; and a newsstand, where he found a paperback novel to hold close to his eyes. He checked his watch and found a bus schedule and checked his watch again. Åsa's bus would show in twenty minutes; with a book and coffee, that was time that he could nimbly kill.

Five minutes later, a voice that was not Åsa's called out his first name. He stared out into the crowd, saw five or six anonymous forms, none of which seemed to be beckoning in his direction. He considered its tenor, its qualities; he tried to identify it, but couldn't identify the speaker. It was the sort of voice that cuts across a room, that skirts other conversations and sources of music to reach a dozen destinations. Still, even with this quality, Will couldn't say who the speaker had been; could not even say with certainty if that speaker had been male or female. Will scanned the lines of the paperback novel and traced the outlines of letters with his lessened vision. He spoke words to himself and heard no other words spoken from the crowd that addressed him. His name was common enough, he knew. He stared at the words in the novel and thought of the frequent cries of "Will" heard in a space such as this and continued to wait.

5

AS HE SAT AND TRIED TO FOCUS ON BLURRED WORDS, Will thought about the end of the group; about Patten's move to academic life and Barrett's sudden devotion to the girlfriend whom he'd dated as the band waned. Had she become Barrett's wife? Will couldn't remember; he remembered a years-long gap in his knowledge of Barrett's life. There had been a letter in 1982 in which there were passing allusions to a pair of shortened marriages. Will hadn't inquired further; it seemed to him that Barrett's life had accumulated enough freshly-settled detritus that to raise the topic would also be to scatter it again. And so he'd gone out, that first time, to meet Barrett on the outskirts of New Haven. They had passed a quiet afternoon in Barrett's apartment, drinking a few of the beers that Will had brought and venturing slightly into Will's own history and halfheartedly playing a few chords together.

The curtains were made from the same set of old sheets that Barrett had used for curtains in their old van, Will noticed. The apartment itself felt something like that same van: insular with intermittent sun, and music a constant presence. The refrigerator hummed along and sometimes tremulously shook the floor. When it came time for Will to leave he embraced his old friend and promised reconnection with Falk and Patten, and that reconciliation had come a year or so later, their first common gathering since their band's final show. He had driven back to New Duchess on that night with a giddiness in his heart, a sense that he had repaired something unaware it needed fixing.

He had paged through a few chapters of the book and slowly recognized that he knew nothing of what had passed in the text. He'd been thinking of them all; of Barrett and Falk and Patten; of how Barrett had always seemed the most unmoored. Of how Falk and Patten had their own life, of how he had his daughter and his studio. He wasn't sure if Barrett even had music these days, or if his sole comfort was the angle of sunlight through a bar's front window and whatever friends or associates greeted him there. Will wondered for how much longer these reunions would last, especially with the new addition of his own necessary two-step. He wondered what Barrett had said to his other friends, and realized that several possibilities came to mind. Will considered them, momentarily lodged between curiosity and a deep fear; the consideration that his old friend might be reprehensible had always sat just outside his field of vision.

He tried again to lower himself back into the novel. The name "Will" or the word "will" hit his ears again, now from a different indistinct shape at some distance from him. He looked over towards it. He squinted, as though that might suddenly restore anything like coherent vision to him. It was an old habit, something that had arisen in childhood. As a child he had thought that this would cure him, that it might substitute for corrective lenses or surgery. It was a tic he returned to over the years, a hearkening back towards an older system of understanding the world. He heard "Will" again—or he heard "will" again. He again searched the crowd even though no faces suddenly came clear, no bodies resolved themselves into forms familiar.

"Hello?" he said. Soon afterwards, he realized that it had been said too softly for anyone not standing beside him.

The sounds of the terminal drew close around him. Closed pockets of conversation; cursory exchanges at the newsstand. College students on a late bus home; high school students exuberant in their just-concluded visits. Late-shift commuters on pay phones, making abbreviated conversations with family or friends, coordinating arrival times and arrangements.

"Hello?" he said again, louder this time, and waited for an answer. He honed in to the din, to the overlap. He hoped for some response, for a word in response to his own before his daughter arrived. He listened for the sound of some familiar voice. All he heard were the echoes of strangers around him; unknown voices issuing from unfamiliar forms.

Will was tired of words; he was tired of the blurredness of his vision and he was exhausted from waiting. He wanted this winter's day and this winter's night to end; he wanted to see Åsa and to see the drive home and to see the simple fact of his home. He stood and lowered the book to his side. He walked to the chart, behind scuffed plastic, where gate assignments for bus lines resided. He pressed his face close in and squinted and saw his destination; heard a security guard's anxious "Sir?" and pulled his face back, murmured a soft apology. The gate's number memorized, Will Morgan began anticipating the sight of his daughter's blurred face, and feel of the journey home. He had a record in his hand, music he longed to hear, and to share. He found the escalator and let it carry him down, away from indistinct lights and blurred sky. Some sort of connection awaited him; that was enough.

SIX

Two Interviews, Seven Years

(1998, 2005)

Interview 1: from Plainsong #3
(Spring 1998)
Interview conducted by Burke Caldecott

I DIDN'T EVEN THINK there was music being made in the northwestern corner of New Jersey, but a band called The Alphanumeric Murders proved me wrong. Friends had talked up their album *Skeleton River*, and when I finally came across a copy, it knocked me on my ass. After seeing them play a show at the Melody Bar in New Brunswick, I asked singer Dean Polis if I could interview him sometime; we conducted this interview a few weeks later.

BC: So what's the scene like up around you in New Dutchess?
DP: Scene? *(laughs)* There aren't a whole lot of bands up here. To the extent that there's a scene around our hometown, it's mostly us and some other bands with people who used to be in our band. Our old bassist Julia's in a pretty great new band nowadays, for instance.

BC: What band?
DP: Annotations.

BC: Oh yeah! They're great.
DP: They are.

BC: Your first album was a really great hardcore record, and then you did Skeleton River, which was a lot weirder. So: are you writing new stuff now? And if so, is it closer to the first one or the second?
DP: We are. Definitely closer to the second album, and maybe even further. I don't know if it's a quote-unquote hardcore record at this point. Maybe it is to our first record what Mr. Bungle is to Faith No More. Does that make sense? Still heavy, still loud, but more carnivalesque.

BC: When you're playing shows, do you find that people like the earlier songs more, or–
DP: It depends. There are plenty of people who like to mosh, and you can't necessarily mosh to anything past the seven inch we did in 1996. I think you could probably debate whether or not we're still a hardcore band, but we're still playing hardcore shows and fests and whatnot, so–draw your own conclusion. We're still filed in that section in various record stores.

BC: Have people tried to dance to the songs on Skeleton River?
DP: Oh yeah. All the time. And sometimes it goes so, so wrong. I mean, most shows, we're focusing on the band and keeping an eye on one another. But sometimes, you just see someone in the crowd who wants to kickbox so, so badly. And it never works. And that guy almost always makes an ass of himself.

BC: Did I see that you're also playing guitar on some songs?
DP: Yeah. That's a new old thing.

BC: What do you mean?
DP: We tried that out years ago, and it didn't totally work. I really like the sound of it, though, and I like bands that have three guitars, so–we'll see where it goes. And I've never been totally comfortable just holding a microphone on stage, so having that is also pretty fun.

BC: You're not holding out the microphone for the sing-alongs?
DP: Exactly. Mostly because we're not writing songs for sing-alongs any more. If we ever did.

BC: What's been the weirdest review you've gotten since Skeleton River came out?
DP: Someone said that we sounded like a prog band. I can't tell if they were being sarcastic or if this was just what we sounded like.

BC: A prog band?
DP: Yeah. Though I think maybe they don't know anything about the

style. It was, like, "Recommended for fans of King Crimson, Dream Theatre, and early Yes."

BC: They did specify "early Yes," so that might suggest a more than passing familiarity with the genre.
DP: True.

BC: I guess that's all I've got. Do you have anything to say in closing?
DP: Be good to your local scene. We don't really have one here, like I said,—you should savor the one you have while it's around.

Interview 2: from Brass Type issue 16 (Winter 2005)

Interview conducted by Burke Caldecott

I FIRST HEARD DEAN POLIS PLAYING MUSIC in a band called The Alphanumeric Murders, one of the weirdest hardcore bands to come out of New Jersey–or maybe the entire United States. They had that same ability to hit you in the gut that plenty of their contemporaries did, but they weren't afraid to send their songs into weirder directions. Maybe it was Polis donning a guitar for the last run of Alphanumerics shows that foreshadowed where his music was going–or maybe not. He recently resurfaced with an album of solo work that sounds nothing like his band, but maintains that same urgency. I talked with him about it over the phone; it was my second time interviewing him, following a conversation for my zine a few years ago.

BC: So in the 90s, you were singing in a hardcore band, and now you're writing music for cellos and pianos. What gives?
DP: I was singing and playing guitar for a lot of that time, too. Just to get that on the record. (*laughs*)

BC: Was that something you'd always done?
DP: Not really.

BC: What else?
DP: Well, it's been a weird year for me. I got divorced–

BC: Is it okay to put that in?
DP: Yeah.

BC: Okay.
DP: So I got divorced earlier this year, and I've been living on my own

for the first time in a while. So I spend a lot of time in my apartment, writing, composing, playing music–

BC: Do you make a living from it?
DP: Kind of? Sometimes I'll temp. Sometimes I'll pick up a touring gig–either tour managing or filling in on guitar for someone for a few weeks of a tour. I make it work. But yeah, I pay my rent.

BC: What ends up inspiring you? I mean, with the Alphanumeric Murders, you had a sense of what the songs were about, even if the lyrics weren't totally literal.
DP: Sometimes I'll be writing something for a particular commission, or a particular collaborator–there's this dance group in Norway I've done a couple of pieces for. Sometimes I'll think about movies or books, too–I'm a big fan of this Canadian writer Robertson Davies, and I'd love to do something inspired by his work. But sometimes when I think about inspiration, I think about my hometown.

BC: Do you still spend a lot of time there?
DP: Every few months I go out there. Sometimes more. My mom lives there, so I visit here sometimes, though she travels a lot. The recording engineer I work with a lot has his studio there, so I spend more time there on some trips than others. It varies, really.

BC: Have you been working with him for a long time?
DP: Oh yeah. He's this guy Will Morgan–he recorded some of the later Alphanumerics stuff. He was in a bunch of weird bands back in the 70s. I keep wishing someone would reissue some of them–it's great. Skronky as hell. Like if Hawkwind and the last Unwound album had a baby, maybe. But they were doing that in 1974. It's so ridiculously ahead of its time.

BC: How does New Dutchess influence you?
DP: Well, it's not always the greatest place. There are a lot of building projects that never got finished; there's this giant hotel in the middle of nowhere that's been unfinished since I was a kid. It's a pain to get

to, and there isn't a lot to do around it—couple of strip malls ten miles away, and that's it. But the rent's cheap. Sometimes I think I should move back there and do all my work from there.

BC: When you're writing music, it seems like everything you've done up until now has been about ten or fifteen minutes long. Do you have ambitions to do something longer?
DP: I don't know. There are a few things that I'd like to try, but it's more writing for different instruments, different ensembles. I don't necessarily need to write a symphony at this point in time, you know?

BC: Do you miss playing with other people?
DP: I mean, I end up playing a lot with the groups—not a ton, because they're much better musicians than me, but I'll plug a guitar in every once in a while.

BC: I guess what I mean is, do you miss being in a band?
DP: Not really. I mean, I was in a band with my friends and it was a lot of fun. And that ran its course, and now it's over. But it's hard to imagine that same chemistry. I don't necessarily want to make that kind of music any more, and right now I'm making the kind of music I want to make. Next month, I might decide that what I really want to do is be in a streetpunk band and write Oi songs, but—for now, it's the cellos and pianos for me.

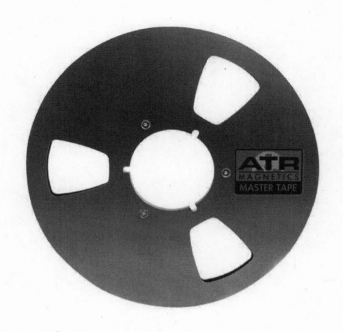

SEVEN

I USED TO THINK LANGUAGE WAS CODE

(2001-2008)

1

ÅSA IN SOLITUDE AND FOG ON ROUTE 46, headlights useless. Not the sort of night in which anyone should be driving, but still she was. The sort of night wherein headlights might illuminate a well-placed bumper or broadcast an impending collision. The sort of night where one should be indoors. She thought about fear and the constant question of why she was on this particular road on this particular night. But these brief spells of detachment had to happen somewhere. Once they had happened when she was base-side and in uniform; they had been a constant throughout her life. Those spells and this road and the house where she'd grown up: that was all.

Sometimes she ended up at bars in New Dutchess or visiting old friends from New Dutchess in bars or restaurants in the area. She was careful to note how they looked at her. It had changed over the years, and she wondered where it might all end up. Sometimes she saw her mother, but those instances were rare. Leap years, mostly: her crossing the Atlantic or her mother making the long trek from Umea to some northeastern airport before a week of travel. Her mother had a knack for finding the most remote Scandinavian towns to visit, and had certain preconditions: rail travel only when she entered the country; cabins near hot springs if at all possible; at least one dance class taken when on American soil. To Åsa this was all normal, or at least the kind of baseline expectation she had for what mothers did.

Tonight the road was familiar but the destination wasn't. She was ten minutes from a hotel halfway between Manhattan and her hometown. She was there to hear stories and record a few and jot down notes and rechart scenes from her past. This was where a conversation at her friend Virgil's memorial had led: a discussion that there were stories that had to be recorded, a secret history that should be documented before more of them fell. And so it began here, or would begin, or might begin. Hotel bars. Funny, she thought. A far cry from all-ages spaces and straightedge t-shirts and crowd singalongs. Two old friends, talking over drinks. It seemed inappropriately restrained.

2

SHE HAD MISSED HER FRIENDS' WEDDING. This was years before the drive in the fog. This was when she was much younger, when Virgil was still around, when they all felt much more in the way of potential. Dean and Marina were wed and she was on the other side of the country, enmeshed in Army life. She vowed that she would take them out to dinner when she returned to New Dutchess, because that was what you did in adult life with your friends, and especially what you did when you missed such massive life events as marriage.

But the next time she returned to her hometown everything seemed lopsided. Dean Polis was off driving the region in long loops and doing field research and making field recordings and—weirder still—periodically hanging out with her father to talk shop. He was still doing homemade demos then; he was still recording things in weird corners of the world, in his apartment or his mother's house, and mixing them all together and wondering what he should sow with them.

For her part, Marina was no less busy than her husband. She was out traveling for work most weeks, at least a day a week in a city that wasn't New York, and was taking classes towards an advanced degree on the side. Åsa was left with admiration for her friend, but also a gnawing sense of time's slippage. For her, time was regimented, on the level of days and on the level of years; in terms of how her days on the base were spent and in terms of the time she had left in that particular way of life. She was unsure of what would come next. She thought, perhaps, that she would travel, though she wasn't quite sure where. The idea of travel, then. That sufficed.

Her work was not related to combat. Language was what she knew, and language became her specialty. She handled translations and occasionally talked with colleagues about codes. She was far from battle. At the time of the absence from her friends' wedding, she lived on one in California; from there, she would go to Texas and then to Germany and then she would be done.

Six months in to her active duty, Virgil Carey began to send her care packages. This was his phrase, not her preferred one. She preferred "a box with things in it," but she had a very particular sense of what a care package was, and while she appreciated Virgil's gesture–savored it, really–this was not what she considered a care package to be. In the box was music: two seven inches and a bunch of CDs and a note: *I got two of these at a show and the rest at a record store in Fords, on my way to New Brunswick one night.*

She emailed him back and asked how things were. Virgil responded with a kind of moderate screed, a manifesto, a description of long hours worked at a bizarre job in midtown Manhattan, some company with a nebulous name ending in dot-com. Åsa read this and wanted to ask, *If you hate it so much why don't you quit?* She understood commitment and she understood that certain things were temporary, but his situation was not comparable to hers, and she left unsure of what to make of Virgil. She wanted to write back a simple phrase: "Virgil, quit." But she didn't. Åsa responded with something else instead, something neutral, some method of changing the subject.

Over the course of their electronic correspondence, Virgil related several things to her. She heard about his weekend journeys to meet up with Dean and Marina and the adventures they had. She heard about Virgil's experience at Dean and Marina's wedding. He heard about how he had spent one longish weekend cat-sitting for them at their apartment on the Lower East Side, but that letter was less about what he had done when he had stayed there and more about the look and feel of the place—how the light looked in the morning, the arrangement of assorted posters from the Alphanumeric Murders days on the walls, the letter they'd left him detailing their preferred haunts in the area, where to get a good beer and where to enjoy a tasty vegan meal. None of them actually were vegan, but their years enmeshed in the hardcore scene had left all of them with a taste for food made under those guidelines. From Virgil's letters she had a full sense of her friends' routines, and very little of Virgil. Something seemed strange; she wanted to see her friend, to see if he had some-how become hollowed-out.

She wanted to ask, straightforwardly, how he was doing. She wanted to ask, perhaps, if he was dating someone, or if he was consid-ering the topic. She remembered a flirtation with an old friend of theirs from the Alphanumerics days. Why not her, she wanted to ask Virgil, but did not. It seemed to her that this might push buttons the wrong way. It seemed to her as though being at a remove from this might cause a kind of further distancing—and presently, Virgil was her one point of connection to the spaces that had made her who she was.

One day she bought a stack of postcards. She sent a postcard to Dean and sent a postcard to Marina and hoped that they would arrive on the same day, lest one of them think the other was being more highly favored. She asked how they were. I hear from Virgil that both of you are busy in New York, she wrote on one. I hear from Virgil that your wedding was amazing; I am incredibly happy for you both, she wrote on the other.

During the day she pored over documents and attempted to wring some nuance from them. On some days she fared better than others.

Eventually Dean wrote back to her. He spoke mostly about the music that he was making. There were a few allusions to the wedding, but largely, it was music shop-talk. She had heard from her father that Dean had some sessions booked, but hadn't inquired further. It seemed strange to her that there had been this connection made between two people who figured so significantly in her life, and she wanted it to remain its own thing, far removed from her. It seemed as though it required a particular kind of balance, and the slightest adjustment to it might make the whole thing shatter.

She could remember Dean attaching short instrumental sketches at the end of mixtapes, though. From the sound of them, she could tell that they were unmastered, but even in that condition they were memorable. She assumed his sessions with her father were some continuation of that, and she eagerly anticipated what might emerge.

Contact with friends from back home in her first year of Army life passed like this, then: correspondence and music, both in fits and starts. It wasn't ideal, but still: contact remained. And, in the background, there was the question of what she was becoming. Did she still feel music's pull as she listened to it? She had developed a feeling of detachment when she looked at language, that separation of meaning from syntax, the notion of seeing multiple possible meanings floating over the text set down before her. A paragraph considered as a game of chess, or of ten games of chess. She began to welcome music in a new way, as the herald of something different, of something her mind could wrap around in a separate fashion. Of something that she could sit back with and feel transported, into a place where words were momentarily rigid.

3

AND SO A NEW YEAR BROKE, and Åsa found herself in a quiet period. It wasn't necessarily meditative, but it didn't lack for meditative qualities. She spent a lot of time thinking about people who had passed out of her life. On the base where she lived she had no close friends. There was camaraderie, certainly, but she had no one here who might act as her confessor, and no one here for whom she might be their confessor.

She began to track things. She opened a notebook and jotted down a list of the significant things in her life. People came first: her father, her mother, her friends, the handful of cousins with whom she'd meaningfully bonded. Then she enumerated a list of places, some close to her hometown and some that were further afield, places where she'd gone when connecting with her mother's side of the family, places where she'd gone to sort out aspects of her life. She spent forty minutes trying to remember all of the names of the town she'd visited on a college-era road trip across New York State, every Gun Club album ever recorded suffusing the car stereo. She thought of places that held sway over her: museums and theaters and music venues and national parks. She thought of objects: a sketchbook and a guitar she bought secondhand in college and a camera. She thought of histories.

On the pages that followed she noted how long it had been since she had last seen each of these things, these places, these people. In the case of people, it varied wildly. She spoke with her father regularly; she exchanged emails with her mother more infrequently. In terms of her friends, Virgil was her most frequent correspondent; her words from Dean and Marina came less often. Other friends had evaporated from her life: some since high school, some since college, some after she'd entered the military. She couldn't tell if this was aging or something more, some sort of political disapproval conveyed through silence.

The chart that emerged was a cause for concern, with traces of isolation and a certain kind of dwindling. She understood her work well; she was good at it. She had been told that she was good at it. She looked at words and dismantled them and tried to find patterns in languages familiar and alien. She saw herself doing that in her own life: as she received letters from Virgil, she began to unmake them and circumvent his hidden meanings and intended meanings and sublimate them into something else.

Åsa wondered if she was somehow becoming aloof. She wondered if her responses were somehow stifling the space of friendship. She wondered if they were simply being carried along by the accumulated energy of routine and familiarity. Notebooks before her, she suddenly felt very alone, and recognized that this was not a feeling she wanted to sustain.

She typed an email to her father in English and typed an email to her mother in Swedish and typed a quick dispatch to Dean in English. There was never slippage. She was proud of this. Apparently she had engaged in it as a child, had created a language between languages that had confounded and delighted both of her parents before their time together came to an end. Her father would sometimes remind her of this, the sole tale from her early childhood that he still enjoyed recounting. Thankfully, this was never in public; this was never a story that he felt compelled to share with others, be they family or friends or the high school boyfriend who'd come over for dinner once or twice.

Will Morgan retained more Swedish than he let on, though he rarely had cause to use it. She had once dredged out a selection of straightedge bands from Umea and scattered CDs before him. "A lot of them come over here now," she said. "Could be an asset, you speaking the language." At the time, her father had shrugged. Swedish had little to offer him nowadays; even so, Åsa still noticed the occasional book with umlauts or overrings on the spine on one of his bookshelves. Did he ever return to these, she wondered, or were they simply mementoes or unlikely decorations of relics of an earlier version of Will?

Here were things to ask here and again, she thought.

4

A YEAR LATER SHE WAS HOME, albeit briefly. She was stationed in Texas, and spent a long weekend in the Northeast. One afternoon she drove to the city to see Dean and Marina. She stood outside of their apartment building and pressed the buzzer. From the speaker came a distorted rattle, which she took for Dean asking who was there. Was it the bitterness of winter that brought impatience with him, that left her wanting him to buzz her in even more quickly, lest she shiver longer? She thought, I should be better than this. And when the door was buzzed open, the squalling sound it made left her disoriented. It was a sound that seemed disjointed from the city around her and the base that she'd left and the town from which she'd driven earlier that day. It continued on even after she'd stepped through the door; Dean, it seemed, was a leaner.

Two flights of stairs brought her to their apartment. The unlocked door sat like a faded blue envelope. And so she walked on in and saw the place: one exposed brick wall, framed photos on the adjoining wall, and a kitchen and a bathroom and an alcove beyond. Dean was alone in there; Marina, he said, was at work drinks or something similar. He indicated a door leading to a balcony. "It's cold as fuck right now," he said, "but when it's warmer out it's great. Glimpses of other lives, like an old movie or something. *Rear Window* minus the wheelchair and the murder." Åsa nodded.

It felt, to her, like truncation. She understood that well enough, and had from an early age. Consider her family's fragmentation when she was young; consider the stories she'd heard from her father about his old band's splintering into dissolute factions. On some level, fragmentation was what she expected from all things.

Though that might have simplified things a bit. Her father now had his annual meetings with his former bandmates; what had been painful had been turned into the stuff of ritual. She could understand that. And now she was working on, perhaps, establishing rituals and regulated meetings of her own. Tonight, with Dean and Marina; tomorrow, in her hometown, with Virgil Carey. She hoped that this would continue, probably in some variation of this form, until Virgil married—which, admittedly, struck her as unlikely—or until she did. This also seemed to her to be unlikely, but still. The onrush of an idea of a new status quo shouldn't have disoriented her, and yet, on some level, it did.

She outlined her daily routine quickly, shrugging aside some questions from Dean with a quick, "You don't want to hear that." After a while she began paying attention to subtle gradation as his face shifted as he spoke and minor shifts in his body language, a kind of distancing. She wondered if he was also quietly pushing himself away, if this casual conversation wasn't also a kind of casual damage to their friendship. She dug in, vowing to be more verbose. She vowed to be more forthcoming about her own history, and extract details of Dean's life along the way. This was less prodding him about married life and its intricacies and more endeavoring to learn about the music he made.

After a while she gleaned that he was being hesitant about this music. He spoke of it in general terms: there was music being made, but anything else, any ambitions pertaining to it, remained mysterious. He alluded to a manager at one point, and that struck her as curious. She let him continue, and wondered when she might hear something new he'd made. She missed the days of hearing rough mixes on old cassettes and having access to alternate versions that never saw the light of day.

And then it came again, the phrase "my manager." And Åsa decided to inquire. "So that," she said. "Not so punk rock." It was a long and running thing that they had, hardly unique among people who'd grown up in punk scenes, and just in their circle, they'd run it through nearly every permutation. This diner isn't so punk rock. Your car? Not very punk rock. That bass amp? Not remotely punk rock, even on its best day.

"I was wondering when you'd say something," said Dean. "I mean—I could maybe argue that it's the most punk thing ever, but." Åsa raised an eyebrow in the universal sign for *go on*. "There's a guy from Future Sound of London who's composing now. And the music for that movie *Pi* was made by someone from Pop Will Eat Itself."

"Sure," said Åsa, "but I never saw Pop Will Eat Itself play in someone's basement."

A key rattled loudly in the lock. That'd be Marina, Åsa thought. She realized that she'd felt the vibrations of her footsteps approach. Buildings were weird like that, strange instruments all their own. Years later, on a visit to New York, she would see an art installation that turned a massive industrial structure into an instrument all its own, and she would remember the sound of Marina's approach and its hesitancy and then the rattle. It was akin to the opening of a sort of punk record she savored, with a clatter of sounds more noise than music, and then the onrush of percussion, and then a beginning.

So they ended up at a French place on First Avenue and they ate and talked. Their conversation largely consisted of trading stories of where mutual friends had ended up: bartending or policing or, in one storied case, the valedictorian of their high school having scored some sort of absurd legal victory in a largely infamous case picked up by the national news and, one report went, optioned for film. Marina mentioned that she'd heard from her brother that the gutted hotel might be completed soon, though she'd heard multiple versions: a hotel or luxury housing or an age-restricted community for the aging souls of northwestern New Jersey. Who could be sure?

Åsa mentioned that she was seeing Virgil the following day. "Tell him not to be such a stranger," Marina said. "He's been remote lately. I don't quite know why." And Dean nodded and said, "I'm worried about him." Åsa watched as their nods seemed to sync up, their intimate proximity slowly folding together.

Late in the meal Dean went to the restroom and Marina went to the restroom and Åsa found herself alone at the table. She heard conversations coming from tables near her: one group was largely engrossed in the smallest details of audio engineering; from a more distant table, she was almost positive, was the arc of what was almost certainly a breakup conversation. She sat there, blissfully unfocused. It emanated from her and eliminated all distractions; she felt entirely alone in this room and also entirely at home in it. She felt normal, felt balanced, for the first time in weeks. She wondered how she'd seemed on the rest of this trip. She wondered what her friends made of her right now, and where this all might go.

In time, Dean and Marina returned. They ordered coffee; when it came, Åsa noted that it had a faint taste of horseradish.

"This is the funny thing," Åsa said. "Half the people I work with these days call me Sue."

Marina raised an eyebrow. "Why's that?"

"My name, I guess," Åsa said. "Can't figure out the overring. They hear it as 'Sue' and they've just started calling me that."

"I mean, you should maybe tell them not to," said Marina.

It was a strange thing for Åsa to deal with. On one hand, yes, that was true. On the other, she enjoyed that demarcation. It let her feel as though one part of her life was fully distinct from the other. That sense of an identity for each walk of her life appealed to her; that sense of being someone when she was in uniform and someone else now.

"Maybe I will," said Åsa. "Maybe I will."

5

AND NOW IT WAS A DAY LATER and Åsa was camped out at a bar, waiting for Virgil. She had sprung for a hotel room; although Dean and Marina had offered to let her stay with them, she had wanted a bit of space to herself. That was also why she wasn't staying in the house where she'd grown up: her father was recording a band that week, and she had little desire to be awakened to the sound of basslines being laid down again and again. She looked at the beer in her hand and shook it a little bit and watched the way its surface changed.

She felt a presence moving in next to her. She turned and saw that it was Virgil. His cheekbones had gone since the last time she'd seen him, she noticed. His eyes seemed lost in his head. "Virgil!" she said warmly. "Sit." He sat. She asked him if he needed a beer and he said that, yes, he did need a beer, and so she hailed the bartender and bought Virgil a beer. He was habitually checking a Blackberry, bricklike fingers hovering over tiny grey keys. "You have downtime, Virgil," she said, and he nodded.

"I mean, sometimes I do," he said. The smile he gave then was more forced; it was a forced smile that called attention to its nature as a forced smile. His second drink of beer brought the glass down to about a third empty. He'd soon lap her, she thought.

"How are Dean and Marina?" he asked. "I don't see much of them."

"Why not?" she asked. "They seem to be eager to see you."

He took a long drink. Thinking, she thought, or reticence to answer. "Well," he said. He drank again; his beer was now down to the dregs. "My schedule is shit, basically. Each of them has a ludicrous schedule. If they weren't married to each other, I don't know how they'd see one another." He sighed. "Sorry, guys. Don't mean to be presumptuous."

He looked at vacant spaces—assumably, placeholders for the absent Dean and Marina. "I mean, we were all hoping we'd get together when you were in town, but that didn't work. Her job kept her uptown and my work kept me off in Williamsburg and it just didn't happen.'" Virgil could do a solid Dean impression, it turned out. "And so instead we have this fragmented reunion," he said. He cleared his throat. His skin, Åsa noted, was cave-dweller pale.

They moved on for dinner: an Irish bar with an office tower looming overhead. Virgil seemed fond of the place. Somewhere in there, they asked after one another's parents. Åsa told him that her father was still, basically, much the same—still recording musicians, still making music at odd hours. "He'll be at it until he can't any more," she said. "It's what he does. It's what he's good at." She tried to imagine Will Morgan at an age where he was unable to do his life's work; it seemed impossible. Though it also seemed to her that her father had never been particularly young: he seemed an old thirty in her oldest memories of him, and now he seemed a decade younger than his actual age (early fifties, for the record) let on. She'd have been fine with that: for him to simply continue on unaging until he left this world.

"Are the musicians mostly local, like Dean and the band, or–"

"They come from all over," Åsa said. "Some of them because they know his recordings. Some because they liked his music. It's starting to float back to the surface. Sometimes he talks about reissues. You never know." Åsa looked at the latest of her beers and saw that it was mostly empty. Her next, she knew, would be her last for the night. "What about your folks?"

"Moving west, they tell me," Virgil said. "Upper middle or southern west; it's not clear yet. But they're going somewhere."

"That's a big move," she said.

"The biggest."

She imagined them, lost in a space that large. Virgil's father, endlessly scanning the horizon; his mother, perpetually preparing for anything that might appear on it. Åsa found it hard to picture any of them outside of New Dutchess, and yet the prospect of any of them, or any generation, who had left returning seemed to her equally strange.

6

BY THE TIME OF ÅSA'S NEXT RETURN to her hometown, the elder Careys had moved to Montana. By that point, Virgil had turned oddly elusive. "Tell me about your ambition," he had emailed her in one missive. She was unsure of how to reply. All she could say for sure was that a career in the Army was not for her; she would not be re-enlisting. Her life now was a daily routine of office work, clad in a uniform. She would have written back to him using the word "regimented," but it felt too closely pitched to her actual life.

Most days she sat before a computer and read things written in languages, some recognizable, some not. She and a dozen others stared at them and sought patterns. She excelled in finding references: tiny subtle traits that could identify an author or unmask someone as they sat and revealed strategies. This was the daily task. This was what was done with regularity. Security clearances were here watchword now. And yet, for all that she felt as though she perceived something beyond what others did, it never struck her as advantageous. It simply was.

Sometimes strange words or phrases invaded her dreams. In these dreams she sat in a bar, sometimes one taken from memory and sometimes one entirely imagined, and would engage in conversation with old friends or paramours. It was only after five minutes or five hours—the sun's arc spanned irregular spaces in her slumber—that she realized that their words followed odd patterns, that the vowels were shifted or the consonants were transposed, or there were letters that served no function in the language of the places where these scenes were set.

One in particular unsettled her: she remembered little save the feeling of the words "this wine is tasty" emanating from her mouth. The phrase seemed both entirely mundane and boldly alien, the kind of command issued by a body-snatching alien in some pulp melodrama as it revealed its sinister origins. It woke her the first time she heard it in dreams, and the disquiet would come again and again and again in the months to come.

She had received a steady flow of messages from old friends in and around her hometown. Talk of solo tours from Dean and talk of work trips from Marina and Virgil's accounts of disquiet in New York, of his search for a house in their home state, of absence. These currents continued to flow, while hers seemed increasingly stifled. It had served its purpose; it had brought her somewhere new. But now she had begun to think about her next move. Not literally; she still had one more relocation in this particular part of it. But afterwards? She was unsure. Perhaps more schooling, perhaps some work, perhaps leisure. Welcome to the unrecorded life.

So she was eating frites in the East Village. She was sitting in the window of a small storefront and enjoying a snack that bordered on decadence, and she saw a frenetic Dean Polis walking down the avenue at increased speed. This was odd, she thought. Dean had told her that he'd be in meetings all day, and yet here he was. She thought that she should hail him, or call him, or make some sort of maneuver towards a rendezvous, but he seemed focused, seemed agitated. It jarred her, seeing a face so familiar and yet removed from its usual context. When anger came, it was in brief bursts; she felt a tension run through her forearms and down through her fingers. After a while, the thought came to her: what the hell, Dean.

Later that night she stood in the crowd at a small venue. She heard guitars played; she saw the drummer's sticks clicking in midair before the moment when the feedback came in. It was a band with ex-members of nobody she knew. They played a cover song; they played an apolitical song. They played several memorable songs. And she stood alone and took it all in. Marina was out of town and Dean had his mysterious excuses and Virgil was somewhere laden with work, or so he said. She wondered if she'd start questioning everything Dean told her from now on. She wondered if she'd start questioning everything everyone told her from now on. She wondered what could be relied upon. Music, she thought; that was about it. And on some level she knew that music would lie to her as well, but that was all right.

The next day, Dean called her. It wasn't quite an apology, but it was something. "I fucked up and I haven't seen anyone in forever," he told her. "It all went bad, Åsa." Since he was using her name for emphasis, she took that to mean that, yes, it had indeed all gone bad. And so she asked the natural question that followed—of just what it was that had gone bad. Dean Polis cleared his throat. "Bad shit," he said. "I'll tell you another time, when it's a story and not something in progress." That was fair, she thought at the time. She could chalk it up after the fact; she could mark down hindsight and let that be that and let it burrow away at her. To make the interrogation. To consider it all in retrospect; to get, as it were, practically forensic on it and the events that would follow.

ÅSA: RECIPROCAL; WELCOMED AND CLOSE TO COLLAPSE. Hari Weldon: formerly emaciated, with hair slowly turning floppy; hovering on one edge of the bed. This was a new thing; this, by its nature, was temporary. They were drawn to one another in ways neither felt comfortable addressing. Neither felt entirely at home in the corner of Texas where they currently resided. Åsa was soon to relocate; Hari hailed from Michigan, a doctor with a fondness for macabre humor and archaic slapstick films. She was still unsure of why they has clicked to the extent that they had. Still, this was a fine way to wake on these ebbing mornings.

For now, she was content to look at the window. The curtains, she noticed, were dusty. Hari was apparently a slacker. Well done, Hari, she thought. She focused in on them more and more. Coarse fabric that still let most of the light through. She watched its weave, so compelled by it that took a few sentences to notice that Hari was speaking. She heard a familiar word, a familiar place. She turned to face him. "Wait," she said. "What about Gothenberg?"

"Oh," he said. "I was saying that I might miss your last week. Because of a conference. A conference in Gothenberg." He was the most langurous medical professional she'd ever encountered. Åsa suspected she'd miss that most when they no longer occupied the same space. Hari was the sort of person whose voice turned flat when speaking with regret. "I'm sorry."

So we're here already, Åsa thought. "It's fine," she said.

"Are you sure?"

"It's fine."

Later: breakfast, and coffee. More coffee than breakfast, truth be told. (Neither Åsa nor Hari did much in the way of eating.) Now Åsa was thinking of ways to take the sting out. This was never meant to be much of anything, but still, the sting was there. "It's funny you say

Gothenberg," she said, and Hari twisted and emitted a small indifferent sound. "Why funny," he said.

"I went there once," she said. "My mom lived there for a while." She didn't meet his eyes. Her right hand wrapped around the lip of the mug until the rising heat riddled her fingers. "But she's not there now," she said.

She couldn't imagine what it was like to be Hari's patient. He was a good listener at times, but could also be a maddeningly neutral one. In some other world, some other version of him was a great detective, a detective who interrogated without being in any way interrogative.

"Where did she go?" Hari finally asked.

"She moved north of there a few years ago. She went with the twins."

Now Hari seemed intrigued. "You have siblings?"

Thank you for the genuine question, she thought. "I have siblings," she said. "Technically half-siblings. I've met them twice. The first time, they were infants, and they were asleep for most of it. The second time it was also brief. I don't know if they remember me. They probably don't. My ex-stepfather didn't want me around them, he said. Said I'd give them weird ideas about language."

"That sounds like bullshit," said Hari.

"Yes," she said. "I'm almost certain it was. But they split up a few years ago—hence the move out of Gothenberg—and I don't think I'll ever see him again." Karl Englar had been his name. He hadn't been married to Malin, Åsa's mother, for long: two years, maybe three. They hadn't courted long. Malin had been married to Will Morgan for longer; still, the evidence of her second marriage was, by one measure, double that of her first.

"Did you like him?"

"No," Åsa said. It was true. He wasn't cold, necessarily, but he was strange. He kept everyone at a distance, it seemed. She wondered about the future years in the life of Karl Englar. She wondered about all of the people who she'd seen for the last time. Karl was, presently, at the top of that list in her mind, but he was far from alone on it. She wondered why all these thoughts of finality were converging in her mind at once. She wasn't fond of it, you could be damn sure of that.

As she drove back home, she zeroed in on an old signal and dug a cassette out of the center of the car and put it in and listened to old songs, songs that were approaching the ten-year mark. She thought about vitality. She thought about time. The songs emanating from her speakers would be well over a decade old when she was out of the service. She thought about listening to the Alphanumerics in the town that they'd all called home and she thought about listening to these songs here, how those familiar emotions seemed to layer themselves over this new landscape. She wondered how they'd fit with the streets and forests of North Dakota. She wondered if she'd feel the same when she listened to it a year from now.

Eighteen months later, she was going through her mail in a small room in North Dakota when she saw a letter with a Texas postmark and Hari's return address on the envelope. Well, this might be awful, she thought. In it was a xerox of a *Rolling Stone* piece on indie rock and classical crossovers; atop the Xerox was a post-it note with "Your hometown, right?" scrawled on it. One of the figures profiled in it was Dean Polis, including a cursory mention of the Alphanumeric Murders. She looked the piece over and thought, This is goddamn strange. That in turn prompted her to realize that she hadn't heard from Dean or Marina in a while. Their correspondence, it seemed, had been a casualty of her move. But that was strange as well. She would renew this, she thought, and sat down before her computer and began to compose messages to them both. After an hour and after a day, no response came from either. Strange, she thought. Both had, historically, been expeditious in their responses. Chalk it up to a bad day, perhaps; chalk it up to travel. Chalk it up to something. She would wait a few days and try again, she told herself.

8

A LITTLE LATER, SHE HAD SOME TIME FOR TRAVEL. She thought about going to New York and she thought about going to Stockholm. She chose New York. She didn't intend for it to be a statement, but perhaps it was.

9

THERE WERE STORIES TO TELL. She felt unsettled. She felt an en-
ervating disquiet. Everything felt alive and everything felt close to
collapse. She couldn't tell, at this point, what was valid and what was
uncertain. She was back in her hometown, and now Virgil Carey lived
five minutes from her childhood home. So that was strange. Her father
had splurged on backyard furniture; also strange, albeit less so. "It's
a business expense," he told her. "Gives the bands somewhere to go
when the weather's nice." She stayed there for a night and then went
to a hotel in the city.

She had been corresponding with Virgil before coming east but
Virgil had been strangely elusive. He had settled in, he told her. He
had bought a house but was no longer working. She couldn't tell if
he'd come in to a windfall or if their hometown's real estate values
had finally cratered. But her hometown didn't seem to be on the verge
of collapse. It seemed to look the way it always looked: that skeletal
potential looming in the distance, the occasional vacant lot, the perennial and unassuming downtown. She understood that, one day, this
might look as though it could become the sort of place photographed
for travel sections and postcards for visitors to send home. For now,
it existed in a perpetual almost.

She drove past Virgil's house. It seemed nice: a newly painted front
porch and a recently-made car in the driveway. All of the lights were
off. She had reservations about her behavior. She wondered if she
should knock or if she should call Virgil or make some other related
inquiry. She wondered where he was. She imagined her own life and
spent altogether too much time considering the state of lights in her
residence at a comparable time of life. Perhaps he was in some inner
fortress; perhaps he was in a room that only faced the backyard, a
desk lamp his sole source of illumination. She had had evenings like
that. Perhaps he was an early sleeper. Perhaps he was experimenting

with circadian rhythms, endeavoring to emulate some other city's time zones through his active hours. Perhaps this was a thing that people did.

She had heard that Virgil's tech work had left him effectively set for life: he had worked for a technology company and been given stock options and had managed to sell those at just the right time to earn a massive windfall. She wondered what that felt like. Admittedly, Virgil's life here was modest, but it also had a sort of security that she'd never really felt. She wondered if she ever would.

After she parked, she called Virgil; it went to voicemail. She left a brief message, reminding him that she was in town and would be in the area for a while longer. She had a feeling that he wouldn't respond. Dean was also unresponsive. Marina, on the other hand, was quick to reply. They met for a drink one evening at bar near Penn Station. As always, Åsa noted, Marina looked poised; she carried herself with a precision a decade beyond her peers.

The essential thing about Marina was a quality that resembled, but was not exactly, discretion. It was something harder to quantify, but in their current conversation, it boiled down to this: Marina did not ask Åsa any questions about the military. She did not ask about life on the base and she did not ask about the war in Afghanistan or the one in Iraq. This was, honestly, reason enough for Åsa to feel increasingly warm feelings about Marina. She had begun to hate being the de facto receipient for any and all questions about American military policy from friends from high school and friends from college and distant cousins. These veered all over the place, though several of her father's cousins would periodically ask her what she thought about the films of Oliver Stone or Michael Moore, a subject on which she had virtually no opinion. She was being asked to provide expert testimony in a field in which she was in no way an expert; she was being asked to analyze the things that she took for granted. Blessedly, Marina's questions were of a very different nature.

That night, Marina looked particularly professional. ("Work lunch," she had said to Åsa earlier.) After their drinks arrived, Åsa began to ask a question and Marina held her hand up hesitantly. "I should probably say this from the outset," she said, and Åsa had a sudden and submersible embrace of where this was going. And thus, she heard Marina say, "Dean and I are separating," and, yes, things did indeed seem to fall into place. Åsa was unsure of what to do next: ask for more details, or change the subject entirely? She determined that she should instead see where Marina's narrative went. This was fine; this was something she knew how to do, and well.

There had not been infidelity, Marina said; not on either side. For her, there had been a slow dissatisfaction with how things had been going: Dean's constant immersion in music, in seclusion and in studios (Marina paused and quickly apologized to Åsa), and a general distancing. Both traveled frequently; their overlap in the same space was increasingly rare. Marina said that things between them had furrowed. Their shared obsessions had begun to splinter. They no longer felt like an essential and impenetrable bulwark against the world's intrusions and invasions. Each felt dedicated, Marina said, but that dedication no longer seemed like a union. They were fighting their own fights, to put it one way. To put it another, they had moved into different keys.

"On paper, we were brilliant," Marina said. She shook her head and finished her drink and ordered another. Åsa listened and wanted to focus in on Marina's words. Even as she tried, some part of her began rehearsing what she might say to Dean. Dean had to be spoken to, and soon; and then, she realized, she would have to figure out where things stood then, if she would end up hewing to one half of this former couple, or try her best to maintain a neutral position. She thought about friendships and neglect. She felt panicked as she ran scenarios in her mind, and she felt a wretched feeling for not giving Marina her undivided attention. But then again, was anyone's attention ever undivided? That was something to think about later, she thought. Soon, there would be time enough for that.

10

THEN CAME WORD OF VIRGIL'S PASSING. She drove out for the funeral, and stayed at her father's house for a few nights. She could hear the sound of dissonant guitars and steady basslines coming from the studio, and she was glad for that, glad that something from years before had persevered. The funeral itself was a small gathering. It was held in the church where Virgil had died, which lent a certain uneasiness to the proceedings. At the same time, where else would it be? Virgil's move towards religiosity had left her a bit aback. He had mentioned it in none of his letters or emails to her, and yet: here were friends of his who knew him only as a member of this community. All told, the crowd at the funeral could be divided into three factions: Virgil's friends from church; Virgil's family, his parents and sister in unspeakable mourning alongside a group of somber cousins; and the aging punks in the room, Åsa and Marina and Dean and a host of Dean's old bandmates.

There was a good bar in the downtown now, and other signs of life there besides: on the skeletal tower of the hotel looming over the town, there were signs of construction, signs that it might finally be made complete. Iterations of Alphanumerics lineups gathered at the bar in strange combinations and closed it down the night of the funeral. Åsa listened to their stories and told some of her own. She heard about what they'd been up to in the years since. She jotted down phone numbers and told them that she was nearby. She began to formulate ideas. She began to think about documenting what they'd made in this town.

Two more years passed. Åsa did not re-enlist. She considered civilian life. She considered graduate programs and private-sector jobs that might make good use of her experience with codes and languages.

In the end, she found an apartment near the Grove Street station in Jersey City and took a job tending bar and thought about her options. She began making phone calls to old friends from basement shows and hall shows and long drives to see bands at venues that had long since vanished: City Gardens and Wetlands and the Bates Lodge and the Melody Bar and countless others.

And so Åsa Morgan came to drive on highways across and down her home state. Sometimes this was late at night and sometimes this was in the middle of the day; sometimes she'd be up with the dawn and would breakfast somewhere in the land of pork roll or in the land of Taylor ham. It wasn't just the Alphanumerics, but a history of the Alphanumerics was her grail–though she also had an idea that Dean would never speak to her for it, though they did exchange the occasional pleasantry via email, periodic checkups on one another, periodic reminders that each was still alive.

One night she drove through the fog on Route 23, heading towards a hotel and a bar. The landscape around her was ostensibly familiar but was, based on the view outside of her car's windows, utterly unknown. Around her was nothing. Around here was mist and the occasional presence of headlights and a glimpse of the pavement that she moved over as she traversed this grey landscape. There was light and there was her body and her car, and there was the sensation of movement; more importantly, there was the feeling of progress.

Åsa continued on her way, awaiting the landscape's ultimate resolution, awaiting her destination, still a few miles off.

EIGHT

THE SAINTED VIGIL CAREY

(2006)

Tape 1
HEY. HEY, DEAN. IT'S VIRGIL.

Remember that one morning when we were driving to the city to see Avail at Wetlands and I said that I wanted to make a solo album and you asked what I'd call it and I said that I'd call it *The Supervillain Tapes*? You didn't laugh. You were always great about things like that. Encouraging me, I mean. Even after all the other things. That might be what stands out the most. You were in my corner, usually, even when you didn't have the time to be.

Shit. This is a weird place to start, isn't it?

Tape 2
So. Hi. Me again.

Weddings are so fucking weird. I saw Feast the other day and he we got to talking and he said that he was pretty close to popping the question, so maybe we'll see each other at that one. I still remember when you and Marina got married. I remember the reception, mostly. Because I fucked up. I had to work at the dot-com where I was working and I couldn't leave the office; I had taken the day off and then I got called and told I needed to be there. So I was in my suit and I was sitting there at work and people kept coming by and making jokes—"What's up, Virgil, you interviewing somewhere today?"

Finally I got done with everything and I couldn't figure out what to do. I circled in my office for a bit and then my boss knocked on the door and told me that I wasn't done yet. I had another half hour ahead of me. So finally I burst out of the door and I took two hundred dollars out of an ATM and flagged a cab and said, "We're going to Jersey." And we went to Jersey. I snuck in to the reception just after the toasts. I ran into Åsa and Diane at the table and they caught me up. I had some beers. That's not too bad, right?

I'm still sorry about that. Fuck. I don't know why I'm telling you this.

Tape 3

Where were we?

Right, so the wedding fiasco happened. Your wedding, my fiasco. I bought the car not long after that. There were a couple of lots near my place in Long Island City, so I didn't have to worry about moving it all the time. I worked a lot of late nights around then. Sometimes I'd be at the office past midnight, past one. The company would give you a voucher for a car service, and sometimes I took it and sometimes I walked to the 7 train and waited and waited and waited. I liked the cars, though. Especially because sometimes they'd be doing work on the 7 and there would be no 7 running late. I'd get a car and sit in the back seat and feel all fancy. Like a captain of industry.

I was working late the night I had to go back to New Dutchess for my mom's birthday. Not absurdly late, but late enough. I made the cutoff for track work. I got home. If I hadn't been so rushed, I'd have stopped for a bite at this pizza place with mirrors all over the walls. It made me feel weird, you know? I'd be eating the pizza—it was good pizza—but I'd feel boxed in, surrounded by myself, surrounded by all these weird-looking guys all eating the same pizza as me.

I went back to my apartment and threw some things in a bag and made for the Midtown Tunnel and made for the Lincoln Tunnel from there. I came through and I headed for 280 and took that to 80 and found a diner somewhere along the way. I sat alone in a little booth, but at least this one didn't have mirrors. I wasn't in there crowding myself. There were a couple of families in there, and a couple of older guys sitting alone and minding their beers near the bar. I looked at them and thought, that's probably me in a couple of years, huh? I got a laugh out of it, I think.

I had a book with me, so I read and I ate my chicken sandwich and my cheese fries. After a while I left and I got back in the car and drove further west on 80. Somewhere along the way I realized I didn't have a card for my mom, and there was no way I could sneak out the following morning and try to find a Hallmark store or something. I knew there were a couple of strip malls a few towns over and I knew that one of them had an all-night grocery store because this was New Jersey and it's in the state charter that we have to have all-night grocery stores in every fourth town.

Sure enough, there was a PathMark, its sign visible from half a mile off. There were a couple of cars in the parking lot. I pulled in and walked out and walked through the grocery store and felt how empty it was. There were some late-night people in there, folks who worked late shifts or insomniacs or whatever. And there was me.

You don't find many good cards in the greeting card section of a super-market, I'll tell you that. But they've got their basics. I found something with glitter all over it. It was a pretty shitty card, to be honest, but my mom didn't seem to mind. When she opened it the next day a shit-ton of glitter fell out and got all over her hand and under her fingernails and all over the carpet. My folks moved to Montana about a year after that. Was the card a mitigating factor? Sometimes I think it was.

Tape 4
Funny story about my mom. There was one time when I came back from a show with a shirt I'd bought from one of the bands playing it. There was a stylized drawing of a copy saluting on the front, and it said, "Bringing down the man." I was wearing it around the house, and she looked at me and kind of raised one eyebrow. I said, what? She said, "Virgil, do you not realize that you are the man?"

Tape 5
I was reading this book about punk in New Brunswick the other day. I wish we'd gone to more shows in New Brunswick. I always heard so

many good things about that place. I didn't go enough. I guess I could still go. But fuck. I don't know anyone there. It'd just be weird. They'd think I was a narc or something.

Fuck. I look like a narc, don't I?

Tape 6

I've been thinking about my old office, for some reason. Notable Objects LLC. The job I was working when I was living in Long Island City was a good job, for all that I complained about it. And I guess I'm complaining about it a little here, too. Smart folks ran the place. Working at a company that ended in a dot com seemed weird back then. "What does it do, Virgil?" my dad asked. He asked it a lot. Sometimes I had an answer for him, sometimes not.

But yeah. I stared at a screen for a lot of hours in a day. But I got stock options, and that worked out pretty well. I knew a lot of people at other companies who didn't, who were unemployed and unemployable around 2000, 2001. Me? I did okay. That's an understatement, I guess.

Tape 7

Every once in a while I'll be sitting on the porch here and I'll see someone jogging by. You ran a lot in high school, right? I ran so much. I remember being a little kid and thinking I was flexing muscles and then I realized it was just fat. That took my kid ego down a ways, sure enough. I keep thinking I'm going to start again.

I see your mom around town sometimes. I wave to her. Sometimes she sees me. Sometimes she nods.

Tape 8

It's funny, the people you see around here. I see Åsa when she's in town, though that isn't all that often. I see her dad a whole lot, though.

Mostly at the supermarket. He favors the late hours, just like I do. It gets me out of the house. I get to see people. I get to stretch my legs. I can walk up and down the aisles while the soft-rock station plays. It's a weird life.

I'm doing a little consulting work with a company in Melbourne. Been keeping Australian hours lately. Trying to, anyway. Trying to get my rhythms to match theirs. I think maybe I'm getting there. I think maybe I will before this ends.

Tape 9

I need to get this all down.

It was a couple of months after the last Alphanumerics show that I took the job at Notable Objects LLC. I started out writing code and then they moved me to working on different systems. I didn't hear from anyone back then. Every once in a while I'd hear from Marina about your place in the city. Every once in a while I'd hear from Åsa where she'd be talking about Army things or whatever. Phone tag. All sorts of phone tag, all of us trying to get our schedules to line up so we could hear a voice on the other end of the line.

But things were always crazy. My hours were crazy, and there was so much give and take: we'd find out that we'd gotten another round of funding, and we'd be chasing something approximating a profit, and it would be frantic, so goddamn frantic.

There was a general sense that people were deluding themselves all around us, that we weren't living in a bubble, that there were plenty of forces outside of anyone's control that could have upended all of us. And so it was a race, to make something solid before the ground fell out from under us. And there was always something more to be done. And so I fell away from everyone.

Tape 10

Those days and weeks and years were all about finding out about certain limits. I realized pretty early that I could subsist on four and a half hours of sleep a night. So if I had to be up at eight thirty for work I could be awake until four. And, pretty much, I was, most every night. I'd watch movies or I'd be on IM, or something like that. Sometimes I'd just get in the car and drive out to a diner somewhere on 280 and get a late meal. I'd be home by two or three. Why not?

Tape 11

So the sleeping late thing. I never really made my peace with what it would do to the weekend. Basically I'd be up at three or four in the afternoon on Saturdays. In January, that meant the sun was already mostly set. I'd see the sky from my window already shifting towards night and I'd be halfway tempted to just roll over and keep sleeping until Sunday.

Eventually, I'd get up and go out and start tramping through the neighborhood looking for food. The bars were key. Most of the restaurants were in that grey zone where they stopped serving one meal at four and didn't start the next until six. So, lunch at four-thirty and dinner at ten or eleven or whatever. It was an okay way of living.

Tape 12

I think it was in early 1999 when you said that we should all meet up and go see Looper play at Tramps on 20th Street. I liked that idea a whole lot, and I got myself a ticket and you ordered tickets for yourself and Marina. We met up at the show and it was charming and weird and great: their singer up on stage playing music and reading lyrics with flashlights mounted on the sides of his glasses. Songs about what Y2K might mean and songs about long-distance relationships.

I think at the time I thought I might still be in some kind of long-distance relationship. I knew people on blogs and stuff. I thought one day I might meet somebody.

Anyway.

You probably remember this, but still. We talked about getting together afterwards, maybe getting a drink somewhere, but you said you had to be up early. You said there was recording to do. I asked what and Marina gave you a look and then you said, "Secret project." And I thought, okay. I thought, so much the better.

Tape 13

Okay, so I'm recording this one in the media room. I'm looking at the records on the shelf. I'm guessing that was the first session you did with Åsa's dad, right? The one at his home studio. I looked at the dates on the compilation Nonesuch released the other year, and it seemed to fit. I always liked those pieces, the keyboard and guitar ones.

You know what? I'm running my hands over these tapes and CDs and records and everything, and my hands look weird. My skin looks weird. I don't know what it is. It feels numb, maybe. I keep looking at my skin and wondering what would happen if I peeled it all off, if there'd be a new me underneath.

My hands look wrong, Dean. That's all I know. Something seems wrong with my body.

Tape 14

Let's bring things back around to music.

Around 1999 and 2000, I tried to make it to more shows. Usually I'd order tickets for something at Bowery Ballroom or Tramps or Knitting Factory and it would be on a Wednesday night and then I'd end up having to work late. I think I probably have unused tickets for a whole bunch of shows around here somewhere.

Tape 15

Sometimes I tried to make it down to ABC No Rio on the weekends to see bands play, but I stopped feeling like I belonged. I wore khakis during the day. I didn't recognize myself. I wore pleated-front khakis and I didn't even care after a while.

I used to spent two hours walking through the Macy's on 34th Street picking out shirts and not even trying them on—it was too late in the night for that—and just ending up with baggier and baggier things. I never quite looked the part. I knew guys who said that the thing that they wore during the day was their costume, and I get that, I totally got that. I knew some guys who could pull style off, who could dress for work and show up at a show in the same thing and look fine. And then there was me. Billowing shirt and pleats. A shitty pirate in bad pants.

Most of the time, I slept through the matinees, though. It didn't even come to being embarrassed. I was just asleep.

Tape 16

Sometimes I'd help the folks I worked with with their projects. Half of the folks at Notable Objects had their own things going on the side. There was a guy named Dalton Tooms who kept talking about this genius idea he had for a movie. It was going to be called *Father Christmas, Meet Mother Hanukah*. I'm pretty sure it was porn. He showed me storyboards once. I helped him make a website. I made some cash. I did little things like that, sometimes in exchange for favors and sometimes to pick up some extra money.

Sometimes people would make it big. Dalton didn't, but Ellen Da Silva? She was another co-worker, and she did really well with her side thing. I'd helped her with that, too. I did okay on that one. I didn't make house money—well, I made house money depending on where you live. Sometimes it was fixing code and sometimes it was building a site and sometimes it was just logic. I think that from an early age, I knew I could be detached.

Tape 17

It was a strange office to work in. There was this sense of forced cama-raderie. The office would go out for open bars and karaoke night. I liked the people well enough, but I could never quite feel up for singing in front of them. There was one guy, though, who was really unassum-ing but would then totally nail a Bee Gees song. It was pretty intense. One of my other coworkers told me that seeing your coworkers sing karaoke was about equal, in his mind, to seeing them naked. I never quite got that.

Tape 18

Is it weird that I'm going to talk about your ex? Sorry.

You know what? It never shocked me that Marina got the best job of us all. She worked crazy hours, like me, but her gig seemed import-ant. It seemed like people cared about what she was up to. She had a *profile*. She had a ton of extra cash. I remember being out with all of you once or twice and her picking up the tab for a nice dinner. That was incredibly nice of her. Generous.

After the wedding, when we did hang out, that's what I remember the most. It would usually be both of us, and I'd ask where Marina was. You'd say, "San Francisco" or "Auckland" or "Madrid." Somewhere amazing. It seemed like she'd managed to avoid the early-twenties shitwork that the rest of us had to do. She had good things ahead of her. That always seemed clear.

Maybe that's saying too much. Maybe she'd criticize me for it. I haven't talked to her in years. I don't know if she'd pick up if I called her now, to be honest. I don't know if we even have mutual friends left. Maybe Åsa.

If I did have one last question to ask her, it would be something like, "Did you feel blessed?" Or, "Were you blessed?" I'm sure she'd fucking slap me. But still, that's where my head went. It's where it always went.

Tape 19

All right, so here's a story about killing time.

Remember how, on one of those weekends when Marina wasn't out of town and you weren't deep in a studio somewhere making music, you called me and said that we should get together? It was the middle of winter, but it was warm for the month. I was, shockingly, up before noon. I heard the phone ringing in the other room and picked it up. Meet at six, you said. There was a bar on Avenue B with Caffrey's on tap and a bunch of Yo La Tengo records on the jukebox. The plan was to meet up at your place and listen to some records and then head over there and have some drinks and maybe do a late dinner, or go our separate ways and then get some dinner.

I decided that I'd kill some time before then. I took the subway to MoMA and spent a couple of hours in the galleries there, letting art face me. I felt miniscule. I liked that. Then I walked to Rockefeller Center and got on board the F and took that downtown to Second Avenue. I got out and saw that it was half past five so I called you from a payphone and said that I was running a little early.

Do you remember this at all? I'm just wondering.

You picked up and told me that you two were actually running a little late and could we meet up at the bar instead, at around nine? And of course I said sure. So I walked up to St. Marks Books and bought some reading material and then I walked back to the Broadway-Lafayette stop and got back on the F and I took that out to Coney Island. Last stop on the line, last stop, there are no more, that was what the conductor said.

I got out and held the book by my side and walked up and down the boardwalk. I looked out at the ocean churning under a darkening sky. It was cold out. The boardwalk was mostly empty, just some kids lurking around looking angry at the world. I wished there was somewhere to kill more time out there, and maybe there was, but I couldn't find it. So I bought a piece of fudge from a guy selling it near the subway station and I ate the fudge and I walked back up and swiped my fare and went back to a train that was stopped in the station and sat there and started reading and waited for the train to head back to Manhattan. I was four pages from the end by the time we got to the right stop.

And I met you all at the bar and we had some good beer and were there late and it was a good night, all in all.

Anyway. I was just wondering. Do you remember any of that? That's my story about killing time.

Tape 20

When work wasn't crazy, which it pretty much was all the time, I looked for places to go on vacation. Mostly in Canada: Ottawa and Toronto and Vancouver and Halifax. I don't know why I was obsessed with Canada. I remember telling one guy I worked with about my plans and he said, "Boy, you must like hockey a lot."

Funny thing is, I don't. My dad loves hockey. He got terribly into the Flyers. Had a giant "Broad Street Bullies" banner hanging in the garage when I was a kid. I tried my best to follow along with the sport. It never took. My dad, though, started going to the Spectrum a couple of times every season. Sometimes he'd be there for work or a class reunion. Sometimes he'd just do the drive. There were a few times when he'd go down in the dead of winter and would end up stuck there, in a cheap hotel for the night. He's told me stories now that I'm older. Getting cornered by conspiracy theorists one time, hearing something moving in the walls on another.

I mean, my dad's done all right over the years. He's gotten involved in alumni things at his college. Keeps joking that I should do the same. "Now that you're a retiree, Virgil." He laughs. He always laughs, and I'm never sure what the laugh means.

Funny thing is, I never made it to Canada during hockey season. Maybe next year.

Tape 21

I don't think I ever expected to be back in New Dutchess. I feel like there's a period in your life when you're old enough to notice adult things about the place where you live but you're already checked out of living there, so you don't care. What that boils down to is, there are plenty of things about our hometown that I'm only noticing now.

There's the walkable area near me, for one thing. I can walk from house to house to house, but there isn't that much else there. If I want to go to a bar, unless I want to start stomping through back yards, it's a car or nothing. There was one place that had regulars, which just meant that I got stares whenever I walked in. I feel too old for the other place that's close by, the one that opened in the downtown.

Right now it feels like this town is like bits of other towns stitched together. Maybe that's what every town is like. And there's still the unbuilt hotel visible whenever you look in its direction. I keep wondering if it's going to collapse one day. That would be fitting, I guess. As long as no one dies when it does.

Tape 22

That same winter I was talking about before, the one where I took the train to Coney Island and back, I remember getting a call from Diane. It was good to hear from her. I think I always had a crush on her, stemming from back in the Alphanumerics days. Didn't ever do anything about it, though. That's okay.

There was some concrete bunker of a space in Greenpoint that did shows for half a second, and a friend of hers was in a band that was playing a show there. So I took the long way. I walked in the bitter-ass cold over the bridge and down from Queens into Brooklyn, and it felt so good. Exercise, I thought. It was a nice idea.

I still had a working Walkman around then. I'd had it fixed once before, when I was in college and there was a dodgy electronics place that got it working again. There was always something great about walking around the city with music on. Like a soundtrack that made the whole experience better. I just remember storming through Queensboro Plaza with sentimental guitars on my headphones and headed to a punk show, feeling really good about life.

Funny thing is, I don't remember anything about the actual show. I remember thinking the band was good but I couldn't tell you anything about their songs. I remember the space being small and warm, but I have no idea where it was. In the back of some storefront, maybe. I went to other shows in the vicinity, but nothing else there. I couldn't even remember the name of it when I thought back on the show. I don't know what that means. Maybe nothing.

Tape 23

Somewhere in there, I had work drinks with some people. It was a Wednesday. I don't remember what the bar was, but I remember it was off Houston Street somewhere. That's weird, right? Remembering how you got somewhere, but not where it is?

I had about two beers and then said my farewells and stopped at a grocery store. I needed some nonperishables. I got a loaf of bread and some cheese and jam and some dried pasta. Pretty standard.

I ended up walking past the Mercury Lounge, and I saw on the sign outside of it that there were some bands playing, and as I looked at the sign I realized I knew one of the bands. I think they had ex-members of somebody I'd seen play a show with the Alphanumerics. Or just a hall show somewhere. It was a band with some people from the scene, is what I'm getting at.

They were starting in ten minutes and I figured, why not. It didn't look too crowded. So I paid ten bucks and showed my ID and walked in. I stood in the back and watched a rock band play while holding a bag of groceries. I was that guy, Dean. I was that ridiculous.

After they finished I got on the subway and went home. The cheese hadn't gone bad.

Tape 24

I always meant to invite you and Marina over for dinner. You two had me over so much, and I appreciated that. I always appreciated that. I think you're a tremendously underappreciated cook, Dean.

I guess that was the other thing I liked about eating over there. You never asked me about work stuff. Which is good, because most of the time, just talking about that got me breaking out in hives, so to speak. It was nice because we could just talk about bands and people we knew and who was doing well and who'd moved where and everything else.

And your place! It felt like a home! My place always felt like somewhere I was crashing for a little while.

Even this house. I own a home. I'm a homeowner! And this feels less like a home than the place you lived in back then. It feels kind of like me remaking the place where I grew up, but failing at it. I got the frames and the family photos and some artwork for the walls. I called my dad and asked his advice on how to lay the house out. He said, "You paid cash for a home at twenty-eight. You tell me."

Tape 25

Around then, when I lived there, there was never much to do in my apartment. In retrospect, I think that's why I never invited you over. Or anyone. There was one bar down the block from me, but it was the kind of place where everyone except for me was a regular, and I'd get weird and menacing looks whenever I walked in.

Maybe I'm remembering that badly. Maybe it was always fine. Either way, I didn't socialize much when I was there. I got take-out and sat at my desk and was mostly online.

Tape 26

I regret not hanging out with you more and I regret not hanging out with Marina more. Sometimes with couples, you're friends with one half or the other half, and sometimes it's an equal thing. I think I thought it was an equal thing and it turned out not to be. It took me a long time to realize that.

I mean, I knew her as long as I knew you. But then, I realize that pretty much every conversation I had with her in our twenties involved you or the Alphanumerics. We didn't really have that much in common any more.

Still, though. That distancing feeling weighs on me, even after everything that happened. Even though I know that, now, she wouldn't actually want me as a friend. Even though I'm pretty sure that you don't, that I'm sending all of these tapes into the void.

I think I'm almost as scared that you actually are listening to all of them. If some communication showed up from you, I'd be terrified to open it. Or if you sent me a tape in trade. Would it just be a single note, ringing out, impossibly loud, deafening me, leaving my ears bleeding and the rest of me a wreck?

Tape 27

I'm trying to focus on the good times.

Do you remember the old performance space Galapagos in Williamsburg? They had this weird indoor pool up front, and on a humid day you'd feel a breeze come off it if you ended up sitting near it. Were we sitting there the night we closed the place out? It was a terrible idea on both of our parts. I had work the next day, and you mentioned that you were recording something somewhere.

Still, it was a good night. We went round for round. You were telling me all the things about what you were working on. I think you were starting to write things for strings then. It felt exciting. It felt like being in at the start of something. Maybe not exactly how I felt when you started the Alphanumerics, but close to it.

I kept asking you if you were doing movie music, I think. And you said, no, this was something bigger.

Tape 28

There was one week early in 2000 when I ended up with some down-time. I had what appeared to be a three-day weekend. It seemed like I wouldn't be called in to the office on the day off or on Saturday or Sunday. So I decided to look at some travel options. It seemed like it was too short notice to book a flight somewhere. I looked at train schedules, to see where I could just sit and ride and not have to think about anything.

I thought about Albany and Buffalo and Pittsburgh. I tried to remember if I knew anyone out there. Friends who I'd met there or people I'd met through you or through folks from college. There had to be something, right?

I should have driven, is what it comes down to. I took the train to Pittsburgh and there were delays along the way. I got there on Saturday night and I had to leave on Sunday morning. My dinner was in a Blimpie in a strip mall. I thought maybe there'd be some music I could see there, but there wasn't. I walked to the river and stared at it for a little while and then it got way too cold for that, so I walked back to my hotel.

When I got back to the office on Tuesday I told the whole thing as a joke. Punchline was, "Well, that's what I get for leaving the tri-state area." Cue the laughs. I told it again and again. That was the joke I had.

Tape 29

My hands still look wrong.

I feel wrong.   I don't know how to describe it. I feel sick.

But I probably deserve it.

Tape 30

I was in a café one night. Next to me was this couple that was clearly in the death throes of being a couple. I've gotten good at sensing that over the years.

I remember one of them looking at the other. It was dead silent in the café other than the two of them talking, because no one wanted to be the asshole who said something that set one of them off. Plates might've been thrown. It would've been ugly.

I couldn't help but watch it all unfold. I'm a really good observer of couples, Dean. I wish I could put it on resumes. "I will be able to tell when you break up." I'm like those dogs who sniff for cancer, but for ugly breakups.

One of them stood up and said to the other person, "You need to stop believing in me." And I thought that was it, that he was just going to walk towards the door and leave. I mean, it seems like the right thing to do in that moment. But he didn't walk away. He sat back down and the two of them just sat there, as silent as the rest of us.

It was pretty awful to watch. Where do you go from there, when you've said something like that? What happens once you've said the thing that's going to eat away at whatever was between the two of you?

Tape 31

So I guess this is where I get to it.

I don't know if you remember this. It was 2002 and I was supposed to hang out with you Fort Greene. I think it wasn't long after you and Marina had left the place near Houston. I was still in Long Island City, taking the G around town when the G was running and spending too much money on cabs when it wasn't.

It was a late night already by then. Marina was traveling for work, like usual, and you were demoing things in the apartment before I got there. At least, I saw the evidence of it: gear strewn around and your microphones out of their cases.

We went from there to a bar and had some drinks. I was asking you how married life was and you said that it was good. You asked me if I'd been dating anyone and I said not really. You told me that I should, that I had a lot of good qualities, and I just nodded, because I wasn't sure what else I should be saying.

We were a couple of rounds into the night. We hadn't eaten much before then, and maybe that's why it happened, we weren't thinking very well. Do you even remember it happening? Were you even aware?

You were talking about your sex life. You said something about sex, and I said that I wouldn't know. You looked at me and paused and said, "What?" And then you said, "Oh." And you didn't bring it up again. You changed the subject. You changed it really quickly.

But still. In the pause right before you said, "What?" I saw your face. You were starting to laugh. You stifled it, but you weren't quite fast enough. You were going to laugh at me. I was telling you something I'd never told anyone before, and you laughed. That's where everything that came next came from.

Tape 32

But hey, let's talk about old shows some more.

Tape 33

I saw some great shows right around then. At least I bought tickets for them. Never went. Never had the time. I could frame all of the tickets and the receipts and put it in one corner of my house and call it art. We could be part of a group show together. You could write music and I'd put up my shitty collages and it would be amazing. Wouldn't it be amazing? You could write an etude for the piccolo. Can you write etudes for the piccolo? Well, I fully trust you could. It would be fun, right? So much fun.

Tape 34

If by some miracle you're listening to this and not the last couple of tapes, I'd advise you to dispose of them unheard. It's a waste. All these tapes, all of them with just a handful of words. I don't even understand it.

But still.

Sometimes I hope you're listening and sometimes I hope you're destroying these without opening them.

Tape 35

I want to basically pause the narrative at this point and make the end of it just, "I was mad." That would work, right? "I was mad at the thing you said and the way you laughed and then I did something awful." That would be fine, right?

Tape 36

Every few weeks I talk with my parents on the phone. Volunteer, they tell me. Give something back to the community. It feels like boilerplate language, if I'm going to be honest. It feels like something any parent of their age could tell any child of my age. They tell me I could teach. They tell me I could work with nonprofits or tutor local kids. I think about that sometimes. I think, it would be a legacy, at least.

I think about the tutoring thing a lot, honestly. I think for a second that I might have something that would be worth passing along. Then I realize that most of my knowledge is outdated, obsolete. The couple of tricks I knew are also basically useless. They've been overtaken by the present day. And that's all right.

I feel like everyone has one good con in them. You work up trust with people and then you can make that evaporate and you hope the payoff was worth it. I had something figured out once. I had a half-way decent plan.

Tape 37

We all have our weak points. We fall for things when we shouldn't. Did I ever tell you about the time I got scammed?

I had an old email address I used at the tail end of college when I realized my college account wouldn't last forever. I got an email there one night from what seemed to be a dating service. It said there was a message there from someone and that I should log in to see it. And I fell for it. It was stupid, I know. I logged in with my password for my email and, yep, it was a hoax. I'd been scammed, and suddenly a whole bunch of people I knew were getting spam from the very same people who'd hoaxed me.

I should have caught on, is what I'm getting at. I'm still haunted by it. Almost ten years later. I'll be sitting in the basement and the exact text of the email that fooled me will run through my head to the exclusion of everything else. It does wonders for my ego. What it taught me was that everyone has their low points. It taught me that everyone wants to believe something. People fall for things all the time. Sometimes that's useful.

Tape 38

Around then–this was early 2002–I had a pretty good idea of when you and Marina were traveling. When you were out of town together and when you were away and when she was away. It was easy enough to figure some things out. Little things you told me; things that you said irritated you about Marina. I'd known you long enough to maybe be able to figure out what might be less than compelling about you, too.

I guess it came down to this: in 2002, if you were getting an email from someone, most people still assumed that person was real.

Tape 39

Here's an anecdote. Not long after I moved here, I started to realize that it was going to be a lot harder to get to the city than I'd thought. There was some party that a whole bunch of people we knew were at– Åsa was even around for it. I wanted to go back, and I realized I couldn't swing it–I had deadlines here and the drive there and back would have left me with all of forty minutes at the actual gathering.

The depressing thing was, I knew this guy Gareth was going to be there. I had wanted to introduce him to Åsa. Not because I wanted to play matchmaker or anything, but because I thought they might get along. They had some things in common. Their dads both played music, they'd lived near some of the same cities.

Fine. I also thought maybe they'd hit it off. I know something about dating. So I kept trying to maneuver them into the same place. I'd text Åsa and tell her to keep an eye out for this guy Gareth, and then I'd text Gareth and ask if he'd met my friend Åsa yet.

It felt like a game. I'd set up the rules and restrictions, and then I'd figured out the winning conditions.

But it also felt like a way I could be present there without actually being there. I know if I had been there, I wouldn't have done anything like actually introduce Åsa and Gareth. I'd just sit in a corner somewhere and watch other people interact.

Remotely, I could effect change. I could help people. I could make a difference. Or at least I could connect two people. In theory I could connect two people.

It didn't work, though. As far as I know, they never actually met.

Tape 40
That idea seemed like something I could pursue further, though.

Tape 41
I started making people. This is what I could do with a lot of free time and an internet connection. Creating a paper trail, so to speak. Giving them histories, letting them spend time in different communities. I think there were five total, and the sixth came not long afterwards.

I could dwell in other skins. There was something great about it. It was a strange process, though. I spent so much time in these different personas, sometimes connecting with people I already knew. Old coworkers or college friends or people I knew from the Alphanumerics days. Trying to make these false friendships feel as real as could be.

I didn't just want to create these insidious voices that would cozy up to people and yes them into oblivion. Sometimes I'd get into fights with people using their voices. We'd fight about movies or politics or video game consoles. Some of them were pricklier than others. I found out which of the people I'd reached out to could handle criticism well really quickly, I'll say that.

But soon their reach expanded, and I was talking with new people, people I didn't already know. Oh, I hated a certain movie? They hated it, too. We had so much to talk about.

Tape 42

I kept these personas at a distance. Some lived in upstate New York. One worked at a bookstore outside of Ithaca. One was going to community college near Baltimore. A couple were spots in New England. As these people made connections, we could dangle the idea of a visit and then pull it back. Finals looming, or a sick relative, or a bad case of food poisoning.

I tried to lay the groundwork early. One of the people I invented had a cousin on the Upper West Side. One wrote about a dream job at the Whitney. So there was the potential for something here.

I kept meticulous records. I had white boards with their schedules and their histories. I dedicated a room to it. Folders everywhere. I needed to make them distinct. I had their Zodiac signs figured out pretty early. Last thing I wanted was a whole pack of Scorpios living in my head.

It was four or five months of this before one of them made contact with you. And another week or so before one of them talked to Marina. I wanted to create trust. I wanted a sense of veracity.

Tape 43

Maybe the most innocuous of all the people I made was this guy named Isaac Defoe, from the middle of nowhere in Wyoming. He was the test balloon. He wasn't there to mess with anyone. He talked music with people—I think he talked about disco records with Marina, and he talked with you about French experimental fiction. My ulterior motives with him were innocent enough. I didn't make him to sow discord. It was more like—I wanted to see how noticed he was. He was the only person I made who was in contact with both of you.

Basically I was wondering if one of you would put it together. If suddenly one or the other of you would email Isaac and say, "Hey, I think you've been in contact with my spouse, too." Or maybe that you'd cut off contact once you realized that. But that never happened. And I never heard from you about it, either. I didn't hear about it from Marina.

Soon enough I figured it was time to give him an ending. So I had him fall for a lady and all of a sudden get religion and renounce everything from his old life. He wished you well in an email and he wished Marina well in an email and that was that.

From there I realized that there was more that I could do. I realized that there was a state that both of you dwelled in that I could press, or adjust, or push in new and different ways.

Tape 44
Half the time I wanted to fuck up. I wanted to botch identities. I wanted to get phrases and backstories confused and tip you or Marina off that something was wrong. Maybe not that I was specifically behind it, but that someone was. That the woman in her mid-thirties emailing you from upstate New York maybe wasn't who you thought she was. That the guy filing dispatches from DIY shows in Baltimore was mostly just pulling other people's scene reports from blogs and message boards and changing the wording here and there. Some days I wanted to play up the inconsistencies. Some days I thought about making an acrostic and seeing if you caught it. But in this case, I wanted it to work. These people were my architecture.

Tape 45
There were times I thought about pulling back the sheet. Of all of these fake lives I'd created sending both of you an email at the same time: "By the way, I don't really exist. This is Virgil Carey."

Even better, maybe: I'd write a long email in that voice I'd created and end it with something only I'd know. Go from the sad farewell to something else. That realization that you'd been fooled. That you'd put your trust in something empty.

Tape 46

I'm getting ahead of myself. I had all of these lives, but I needed a finale.

Even now, I think I did an excellent job of making crushable humans for both you and Marina.

After some of these conversations had gone on for a while, I started to notice an effect. I got the impression from talking to you that there were problems in the marriage. I bided my time. I peppered certain emails from certain faces with these notes of sympathy. I tried to see what I could find. Sympathetic ears you and Marina could each lean into.

And somewhere in there I started suggesting meetings. To both of you. "I know this might be forward, but." I kept finding reasons to schedule conversations with you both and then I came up with valid reasons to cancel those conversations. Marina went so far as to buy a train ticket. The pulling in and the pulling back. You'd each met new people. You'd each fallen out of love with the other.

I heard she was moving out from you and I gradually started watching the fault lines. I knew I was going to pull back more; I know I needed to start phasing these people out of your lives. And so I did: one of them ended up "meeting someone." Someone else took a nonprofit job on another continent. Another fell into a deep depression.

These fake people faded from your lives and you and Marina moved into new homes and divorced and I was all set. I had gone and done it.

Tape 47

When I heard Marina had moved out, I sent her a couple of emails saying how sad I was about the whole thing. About how I wished I could be there for her more than I was. I made excuses. Something weird and petty. That, I think, was when she ceased to be friends with me. Which is what I wanted, I guess, that further isolation.

Things went much the same with both of us.

Tape 48
Åsa tells me you're doing well. Hell, I see that you're doing well when I read about music.

She tells me Marina's also doing incredibly well. Successful, she's met a great guy. Maybe what I did was the right thing. Can't imagine it was, though.

Tape 49
It's the funniest thing. I was out at the grocery store last night. It was late. Two in the morning, maybe. Just me and my shopping cart. I had one with a fucked-up wheel, and so it kept dragging and making this horrible racket. Not the best thing ever.

I was walking and I saw Åsa's dad. He was picking up things. Healthy things. Some carrots, some juice, a bottle of agave sweetener. I said, "Hi, Mr. Morgan," and he looked at me and nodded. I don't know if he remembered me or if he though I was someone else or if he'd just had a long day. If he'd had a hat on he'd have tipped it, I think. He's that kind of guy.

And I walked around a little more. I spend way too much time in the supermarket these days. I don't really get a lot. I live a pretty monastic existence here, Dean. But still. It's nice to see the world. The bread aisle and the milk aisle and the pasta sauces and the weird ice cream cakes.

Anyway, I passed some more time there and then I thought I was alone again, just me and the skeleton crew restocking shelves and working at the front register. And I looked up and I saw your mom. She was there, looking very fancy, looking like she'd just come from some sort of society event. She was picking up some coffee or some tea, or at least she was in that aisle.

I was going to say hello to her, too. It seemed like the polite thing to do. Say hi and ask after you and perhaps tell her to pass along my greetings. She must have heard me coming, because of the aforementioned broken wheel, and she turned, and she looked at me. She gave me this very unpleasant look. It seemed to say that she understood what I had done to you. Whether or not you knew, she knew. And I couldn't tell if she'd gleaned it in that moment just from looking in my eye or if she'd known for years.

I caught that, "Hello, Mrs. Polis" in my throat and just managed to exhale a little bit and then I turned around and went the other way. I sat in the fish section for a little while, debating whether to buy a flounder filet as my alibi.

Eventually, I went to go pay and didn't see her on my way to the cash registers, and I didn't see another car in the parking lot. So I'm pretty sure I was safe. And I went home and stayed up for a couple more hours and went to bed just as the morning light was starting to filter in.

Tape 50

I still wonder when I'll get a call, or an email, or a series of staccato knocks at the door.

Clearly you have not been listening to these tapes. Oh well. I wonder when you will. If you will. Will it be some snowy weekend, when you don't feel inspired. Or maybe you're throwing them away as you get them, or taping over them. Maybe you're using them for demos, or for wallpaper. You're not reaching out. I'm probably never going to know.

I don't feel good at all, Dean. There is something very wrong with me, and I don't think I care.

I'm not doing all of this—these tapes, this narrative—to know what you think. I want you to know what I did. But ultimately, there's not much I can do about that. I can't drive to your place and leave these playing on your front stoop. Or just stand there, pushing these hands against the door incessantly, waiting for you. Waiting for something.

I sometimes wonder what your face will look like when you see me. Will I get contempt or surprise or sorrow? It's a moot point. Our time is done, I think. It was done if you didn't listen to the tapes, and if you did listen to the tapes? If you did, I can't imagine you'd want to see me. So there. That does it, right?

Tape 51

It's been a few months since I did one of these.

I woke up this morning and thought about walking through the old part of town. I'm trying to do that more. I'm trying to feel like a part of something again. I still don't. Maybe I never will. I feel like an annex or a parasite depending on the day. Maybe the best I can hope for is something symbiotic with this town and the people in it. To be different from them but somehow of them. I don't know.

I used to fit in here. I used to feel holidays looming and know that I had that same shared routine with the people around me. I knew that we all had that weird shell of a building above us and the same joke of a downtown for shopping and the same strip malls and supermarkets five, ten, fifteen miles away. But I don't feel that sense of community any more. I don't know if I outgrew it or if I moved away from it or if you just can't get at it now.

I feel like I'm stuck in a bad copy of the place where we grew up. I'll still see familiar people, sure, but mostly it's just me, watching it all go bad. There's still trying to be done, but—

I wish I could say more. I wish I had more to say. I think back on what I've done, and I never knew I could hate so much. I wish I hadn't set it all in motion. I'm sorry.

NINE

REUNION TOUR

(AFTER)

1

A Dean Polis Cover Version

NOT FOR THE FIRST TIME, Dean Polis wondered what the hell he was doing.

It was an autumn evening. The drive from Kensington took him an hour and a half. All that rang through his car as he drove was the sound of records he'd bought at 23. He feared calcifying. He feared that moment when he'd be overtaken by his own past, not that the practice space that was his destination on the following day was exactly a counterargument against calcification. Still, there was room for a stop in his travels.

The morning after his concert at the cathedral he'd awakened to an email from Åsa among the missives in his inbox. She'd sent it to an address he hadn't used in years, and that fact disoriented him more than he'd expected. It seemed indicative of some greater disconnect. Not for the first time, he wished his past wasn't so elusive. He wished he had someone with whom he could speak about that loss of control, of that accompaniment to aging, that slow recognition that certain acts couldn't be redone, that certain deeds were permanent.

Not for the first time, he missed Virgil Carey. Even now.

Was it selfish to regard a specific friend as one's own confessor? Probably. But for a time in their friendship, Virgil had seemed to be the one with his life exemplifying togetherness. He had had a steady, lucrative job; he had become a homeowner early on. He had earned enough to retire before he was thirty. And then he had gone back to their hometown; he had returned to an isolated state. That was how it had seemed, anyway, before the tapes arrived.

In the car, he cued up an A-Frames album a friend from Seattle had given him a few years earlier. It was no longer a new album, but it was less than a decade old, and this gave Dean some measure of satisfaction. The guitars hit him jaggedly. He borrowed that energy as he drove the car onto another New Jersey highway towards the hotel. Staying in his hometown didn't seem like an option: his mother had moved to a smaller home years ago, and although construction was nearly complete on the once-skeletal hotel, it had not yet opened for business.

Fog had set in by the time he'd reached the western third of the state. He felt nebulous, as if he was the only thing on the road. Not much longer now, he told himself, and listened to the guitars endlessly chiming.

He wondered when he'd be able to see the hotel. He wondered what it might look like. Panos had sent him news that it was nearly open. One day, perhaps, he would sleep there and carry out a task that left his heart heavy.

Åsa was at the hotel bar when Dean arrived. He seemed displaced from some other, more interesting hotel. He carried no suitcase. She assumed that he had either left it in his car or checked in to his room already. Whatever wing he was in, she hoped it was far from her. Conversing with Dean was fine; an awkward run-in at the vending machines or a salacious or desperate knock on her door were not.

She wasn't sure how this would go. Was it a rescue of their friendship or some last attempt to salvage something from it? She wondered if this would be the final rupture. She was still unsure what to make of the Dean who approached. She still remembered the sting of hearing their dead friend's voice emanating from speakers that night at the concert. Dean had alluded in emails that there was more to it than a simple hijacking of a voice, but had been vague on the specifics.

He raised his hand in greeting. He seemed out of practice in being awkward. Had Dean ever been awkward, Åsa wondered, or had charm always been his lot? Did singing in a band give you charisma, or did the naturally charismatic gravitate towards the microphone? She remembered him in the cathedral, surrounded by musicians byt not disappearing into their midst. He'd seemed to be the heart of the operation, the tactile fuel for the process. She had looked up other footage of him, had seen him in other ensembles, always doing the same thing. That attempt to disappear, that attempt to blend in, and that utter inability to do so. Perhaps masks or shrouds would be next. She would pay a not insignificant part of her savings to witness Dean Polis vanish into full-on eccentricity, donning a cloak and a monster mask, and holding on tight to some flawed notion of art.

"So," Åsa said. He nodded, and they sat.

"Well," said Dean. "I hear you've been collecting stories."

"I collected most of them a while ago," she said. "I'm putting them together now."

"Who are you putting them together for?"

"I don't know yet," said Åsa. "It seemed like a history that needed telling."

"So it's nostalgia," said Dean.

"Nostalgia is easy," Åsa said. Were they talking around the subject, she wondered. "I can't say I miss being twenty. I cringe, more often than not. But still, I like the idea of having all those stories in one place." She looked him in the eye. "I still feel like it misses your voice."

He sighed. "I have a weird relationship with my own past."

No shit, Dean, she thought. "That's an understatement," she said.

He looked off to one side and took a drink. "Well," he said. "Would it be too late to talk, to add some things?"

She looked at him. She took a drink and took her time. She would, in fact, make him wait just a little. Poker face, she thought. "It would not be too late."

He exhaled just a little bit. His body language seemed relaxed. "Okay. Okay, then," he said. "That's good."

She looked him in the eye. "So I do have one question. You tell me you're going to our hometown, but—it's not to record with my dad. So, family stuff?"

"Not quite," he said. "It's funny—your dad and Panos were, up until recently, the only folks from back home I was talking to on a regular basis. But that's changed."

She looked at him. "What do you mean," she said. "It's not like you're reuniting the band or anything."

"Funny you should say that," Dean said.

2
The Return of the
Alphanumeric Murders

AT THE HOTEL ÅSA HAD ASKED DEAN if the Alphanumerics were writing new songs. He had shaken his head. She had wanted to discuss this with him further, had wanted to explore her unified theory of band reunions, but had pulled back at the last minute. This was, after all, their first time speaking in years. Why ruin it?

She wondered who Dean would be after this. Was this one show only, she had asked him. He shook his head. More than that, he had said. A few shows, some festival appearances. Apparently the Alphanumeric Murders had become something of a legend. He said something about reissues of their albums; he said something about there being interest in the oral history she had assembled. She said, give me some time to think on that. He had nodded.

She had asked about his compositions: were they on hold? He had said no. She opened a beer and sat at the table and flipped through a magazine. Dean had told her that it was strange, that it felt like inhabiting his younger skin, or of playing a role. She could understand that. She wondered where it might lead. He had said that he might rewrite some lyrics, rethink some turns of phrase that now made him cringe. She could understand that, too.

Would he stand on larger stages than any of those the Alphanumeric Murders had ever occupied? It seemed likely. Would he look out and see crowds who hadn't hit puberty when his band was previously active? She imagined a revitalized Dean Polis, or a Dean playing himself; a Dean Polis cover version. She would see the result soon enough. Their first show, apparently, was in three months' time—early in the new year. She would certainly be there, to see if it was a triumph or a train wreck. Or maybe both, depending on your angle.

The practice space, then. The instruments, some of them old and some still shining. The songs and the rhythms that had, it seemed, never left him. In the moment, it seemed to Dean that this was the backbone of all the music that he had written since. He was sure he would think better of this idea before long, but for now it was a time to savor it. Later he would ascribe this sentiment to an unfamiliar rush, his old muscles no longer dormant. But for now he felt immersed n the moment and the sense of it all. It seemed to him to be a kind of home.

The rest of the band, in its 1996 configuration, had practiced together twice before. "The structures," Panos had told him. "We needed to make sure those were there before we moved on." It was a strange lineup; it was a version of the band that didn't correspond with any particular era. The reception that their albums had had over the years was intriguing; each had its own champions, and the set list they had been devising drew equally from all periods of the group's life. It was malleable enough that this could work, he thought.

Dean had a vision of the returned Alphanumerics charging back into life with a new project without him, once these shows had run their course. He could see it happen. He joked to Panos once, "I've given you all a common enemy," and had laughed. So had Panos, in theory, and Dean wondered for a moment just how the reunion was going to pan out.

There was certainly downtime. There was a writer friend of his who lived south of there, in another town on the banks of the Delaware near New Hope, and Dean had set up shop in his apartment when the writer was out on trips to adjunct assignments and assorted residencies. Not for the first time, Dean realized that he was now friends with proper educators, with people with families.

He bought flowers once and set them in his writer friend's kitchen. One day he returned from practice to find flies walking over them. The flowers soon sank into the trash can below the sink, and Dean resolved to impart future décor that wouldn't rot. He sat and watched the river and thought of compositions, thought of notes, thought of what this immersion in his own history might bring.

Virgil had left Dean his ashes, with the instruction to disperse them in their shared hometown. Dean had been carrying them with him on these trips out, had intended to do this task months before, but the timing never seemed right; the location never seemed ideal. And so this nondescript urn was his primary companion, along with the questions that accompanied it.

One night when he was staying there he awoke, and for a split second he believed that it was morning, felt fully refreshed. And then he knew that it was not. He saw no sunlight coming through the gap in the curtains in the bedroom, only shadows playing on the walls around him. He inched his body up in the bed, not quite to a seated position, but something more primed for motion. And as he lay there, eyes alert and unwise, he felt it overtake him, the sense of something that had gone irreparably wrong, and had come to rest on him. There seemed only one thing to do, and as he opened his mouth, he wondered what would contain the sound of his scream.

3
Åsa Morgan and the Ashes

Asa was at the last Alphanumeric Murders Practice before the reunited lineup's first show. This was in the early months of 2009. There was a small group of them there: significant others and old friends and a couple of curiosity-seekers who'd charmed their way in. It felt somewhat like old times and somewhat different, and that was fine by her. The band was testing out its set; they were curious as to whether juxtaposing songs from different periods made more sense than a more chronological approach, and thus they'd sought something of an audience.

After it was over a few of them drove to the bar in the lobby of the long-dormant hotel, finally opened after all these decades. It was oddly elegant; spotlights shone up the sides and lent it a strange art deco sense of glamor. If it seemed displaced, it didn't seem to have an adverse effect on the bookings. The place, to Åsa's eyes, was packed.

Several of those who'd traveled for the practice were staying there: Åsa herself was on the tenth floor, and Dean had a room at the top of things. It was a pleasant hotel, all in all. It was designed well and sprawled impressively. "It's the first night I've spent in New Dutchess in years," Dean said at the bar.

"Top floor must've cost a fortune," Panos said as they finished their last drink of the night.

Dean cleared his throat and said, "Well. I had a reason." It was down to four of them: Panos and Dean and Diane Ost and Åsa. Dean explained his line of thought to them and they nodded. And they filed into the elevator and took it to the top floor. Dean led them to his room and swiped a keycard and opened the door. They walked in and took in the room's décor; it was restrained, muted, and just a little bit askew. Åsa liked the look of it.

A suitcase rested on the bed, unopened, and an urn rested on the small desk. Dean opened the door to the balcony and led them onto it, urn in hand.

"Seems right," he said, and his old friends nodded. He opened the urn and released Virgil Carey's ashes into the wind that carried them over the river and past what remained of the town of New Dutchess. For a brief moment Åsa thought she saw, in the lights, the form of Virgil falling slowly and gently towards the earth, an echo of her friend for a brief moment, a still form plummeting towards the earth and then suffusing the place; a sort of christening. And then the ashes were out of sight and the form of Virgil was gone and there was only the four of them standing there, looking over a town that had been remade, new ghosts and old songs wandering the streets.